Portal of Creation

Book One in the Series

The Fractal Edge of Universal Mind - The Jewel Glittering in Hyperspace.

Andrew Rand Brassil

Copyright © 2011.
Front Cover - Shaun Friesen.

ISBN: 978-1-4709-5301-0

Dedicated to my wife Lisa for all her loving support.

Special thanks to Shaun Friesen for technical and artistic assistance.

Contents   Page

"There is a gigantic portal - a pathway of entry onto your planet - that certain creator gods have owned and occupied for 300,000 years. There have been raids, there have been fights, there have been all kinds of things over this portal. Through this portal, the frequency of mankind can be controlled - it is not the only portal - there are many other portals although this is the prime portal that is being fought over at this time. Those creator gods who were here 300,000 years ago are returning. They are still in existence.

They do not live, operate, or exist under the same laws that you do. In other words, 300,000 years is not too long to live for them - do you understand this? This is your time sector, not theirs. They are very interesting beings. They have helped develop your civilization. They have helped destroy your civilization. Even amongst themselves they argue and fight. Believe it or not, creator gods do this. They are losing control of the planet, so they go back to their prime portal, and they create fear and chaos in their portal area, because that is their nest."

Barbara Marciniak - The Pleiadians

Introduction - Genesis Revisited

Queen Antu lay on her side while Two servants ritually cleaned her feet and hands. Her son Enki stood in front of her royal dais; the only person in the kingdom besides his father, not forced to kneel before her. Enki was in a fearsome temper, his jaw and fists clenching in time with his inhalations, as he paused between sentences. Enormous muscles flexed on his seven foot tall broad shouldered frame, thick locks of dark hair visibly coruscating with his pulsing rage.

Dressed in the white toga of the Senate, the gold royal insignia pin clasped at his left shoulder and a fine woven gold belt round his waist, his diplomacy on matters of state was, in this instance, a stark contrast to his godlike appearance. "This is completely outrageous! We can ill afford a full expedition back to Earth at this time. Humanity has come a long way in the last thousand years. They have again tamed the power of the atom and their internal bickering is at an all time high. They have forgotten the incident at Babel. They have forgotten the nuclear wastelands of Sodom and Gomorra. Enlil must show restraint this time. You must talk to father."

"Enki, my son," said the queen, her voice low and resonant echoing in the large room, "I know you love the

Earthlings and have always been good to them, however, we need to take the opportunity of their galactic alignment to further our own goals. Earth is a backwater planet. Our emissaries there report all is unfolding according to plan." One of the servants scrubbing Antu's cuticles caught the tool under the huge woman's fingernail, and was knocked with a reflexive backhand slap from the dais onto the floor. Momentarily dazed, the young servant lay sprawled upon the cold stone before being able to compose herself. Kneeling now in silence, she awaited her fate. Antu glared at the servant girl, but took advantage of her freed hand to heft a large knuckle of smoked meat from the gold platter laying by her voluminous bosom, and held it to her ruddy nose. Closing her eyes she savoured the smell of aromatic herbs with which the meat had been basted, before tearing off a sizable chunk of the pink flesh with her diamond tipped incisors. Enki stood there contemplating his next gambit, oblivious to the scene which played out before him.

Antu finished with the greasy bone and dropped it into the gold bowl used for her scraps. After wiping her hands on a scented hand towel she repositioned an animal pelt cushion under her ribcage and looked at her son.

"Enki. Take this girl with you and have some fun," she cajoled, pointing her foot at the servant kneeling with her head bowed. "You have spent forever protecting your Earthling subjects from their fate. Earth's Tribulation was ordained before we even perfected their lineage. Look instead to make peace with Enlil; for he is also your father's son. You are the eldest, and it falls to you to make things right between the two of you, before our own Ascension." She raised a massive arm to halt his response and continued, "I will then persuade your father to let you go back to Earth and complete the mission you so deeply cherish." Enki bowed to his mother, turned on his heel and clicked his fingers: the order to have the servant girl taken to his quarters.

Antu rolled onto her back and stared up through the crystal apex of her pyramid, the two suns almost aligned above her. She thought back to her time on Earth all those millennia ago. *They were exciting times*, she mused, *the time of one's youth*. The remaining servant girl, who had been cleaning Antu's feet, gathered the tools of her trade and backed out slowly, leaving the queen to her thoughts.

That evening Enki and Enlil met at their father's pyramid in a secret chamber below ground. Even though their respect for one another was undeniable, their differences of opinion on matters of state were legendary. Enki the diplomat, Enlil the warrior. They ruled their kingdoms as differently as night is to day.

Naldi stood on a ledge perched precariously on the side of a jagged outcrop of granite, looking up into a bright, pale orange-blue sky as a gentle breeze willowed hair long dark hair. *This doesn't seem right,* she thought, blinded by the light of the two suns beating harshly on her face. Gazing out through a narrow gap of rocks, her dark brown almond shaped eyes slowly adjusting to the brightness of the day, she saw only bushland extending into the distance of the landscape below. She could hear men talking somewhere beneath her and decided to make contact with them. Climbing down the side of the mountain, which contained the portal she had just exited, Naldi thought about the other portals and her encounter with the tribe of dark skinned people whose customs were so different from her own.

As she emerged from a copse of wind-swept trees not much taller than herself on the opposite side of the mountain summit, she saw a vista that took her breath away. Glinting in the bright sunlight were the irregular shapes of countless buildings; a cityscape her mind had difficulty comprehending. Emitting a low thrumming sound as it passed, a craft unlike anything she had ever seen flying over her home in the mountains of Nepal, slowly made its way to a landing pad she could vaguely discern in the valley below. *I wish Bon Chen was here to see this,* she thought, as she continued her descent. Naldi was having a difficult time making her way down amongst the massive outcrops of granite, and hearing a shout coming from her right, looked over to see a man holding an iridescent blue light pointed at her chest. The man's clothes seemed to be merging with his surroundings and she found it very difficult to focus on him. He gestured for her to come to him, just as several other men also carrying the bright blue lights appeared behind him.

The four men escorted Naldi back into the mountain through a wide tunnel, and descending via a winding staircase cut directly into the natural stone, made their way to the base. Everything about the men seemed familiar but she could not place which country she might be in. *It could be Egypt; but the Egypt of three thousand years ago. Is it possible I have gone back in time?* Walking behind two of the men she could see their uniforms were made from a series of small flat metallic pieces, each about the size of a peach stone, layered like fish scales. They wore close fitting helmets made of the same shiny material but these pieces were about half the size of the ones on their tunics. Around their waists were fastened wide dark brown leather belts. Leather sandals, with three sturdy straps and buckles securing them behind their calves, protected their feet and shins. *They look like Roman gladiators.* Each of the men carried a short black club, which glowed with the bright blue light emanating from one end. She wasn't positive, but believed she could hear the clubs emitting a very high pitch sound. Their tunics made swishing sounds as they walked.

Reaching the base of the mountain, Naldi was directed to enter and sit in a small vehicle with no wheels, similar to the large one she had seen fly past her earlier. A low humming vibration increasing in pitch was starting to make her feel uncomfortable until, forcibly thrust back into her seat, they sped off towards the city centre. Naldi had visited Katmandu when she was a girl and recalled the amazement she felt when she first saw it spread out before her, in the valley surrounded by the four great mountains. As they traveled through the city streets, she recalled her favourite books from school, which showed artistic recreations of ancient metropolis' like Egypt, Babylon, Rome and Greece. The books described how the peoples of those cities lived. *This is definitely more like Egypt, Greece or Rome than Katmandu,* she concluded.

After arriving in front of a small pyramid covered in polished limestone, Naldi was led from the vehicle through a massive archway, guarded by sentries in golden tunics similar to the outfits her escorts wore, through an ante chamber flanked by two more sentries, and then into the central room. On a large wooden dais directly below the apex of the pyramid, lay an extremely corpulent woman clad in a white toga. The woman stared at Naldi as she was lead towards her dais across the marble floor; the sentries' sandals making a sharp slapping sound as they walked. Naldi scanned the raised platform and saw a large gold platter burdened with foods, many of which she could not identify. She noticed the woman's toga was fastened at the shoulder with a thick gold pin and that a delicate circlet of gold sat atop her large, conical shaped, bald head. Not knowing whether to return the woman's gaze or look to the floor as her escorts were doing, Naldi looked up behind the woman and saw an unusual image carved into the sloping wall beyond the dais. Before she had time to comprehend the image, a hand pressed her head painfully downwards as she was forced to kneel on the floor. Her escorts stopped and dropped to one knee, then the man who had originally called out to Naldi on the mountainside, spoke a few words deferentially to the woman laying before them while Naldi kept her gaze fixed on the polished marble.

Naldi felt a clawing sensation in her mind. She pictured white-hot metal rods burning holes into thin red silk draperies as words started to slice into her thoughts. *"You have come home my child. Back to my loving embrace."* The voice was cold as ice and as ancient as stone. *"Your tribe is a persistent one. Do they forget the legends of your creators?"* Naldi felt fear grip the pit of her stomach, but was overwhelmed with a sense of euphoria as visions of her ancestors standing before this woman, stretched off into countless time. Before Naldi could say the words forming in her mind, the woman's voice resounded in her head, *"Yes, they have all visited me. Your people are not long lived like us but we designed you that way for a reason. You will live your life here and we will find you a mate; you are a pretty one. You will want for nothing. Well, nothing but your desire to return to your home but this I forbid."* The guards stood, turned and lead Naldi back outside to the vehicle. As they sped away through the city, Naldi burst into tears. Yes, she knew the creation stories of the gods who walked amongst the first peoples on Earth but had grown up thinking they were only myth. The tales of primitive peoples trying to make sense of their world.

They arrived in front of a stone building with two fluted columns supporting an arch of polished granite. Carved in exquisite detail into the stone above the archway, two winged creatures holding a sphere in their talons, long scaly tails curving like snakes behind them, made a menacing sight. Their heads were turned upwards and away from each other. Their enormous beaks, filled with the teeth of wolves, snarled at the heavens. Their massive wings spread as their claws ripped the orb asunder. Still looking up as she was lead between the pillars, Naldi saw that the orb was planet Earth and felt the constriction of fear grip her again.

In a room lit dimly by several of the blue lights mounted in sconces on the walls, Naldi, held between her two escorts, her left arm forced out in front of her, was branded on the wrist. The searing pain ended abruptly as her stinging flesh was moved beneath a chillingly cold blue glow. Emotional fatigue as well as mental confusion had drained her to a point of queasiness and she fainted.

Naldi woke in a small room, laying on a bed of soft animal pelts. For the briefest of moments she thought she was back in her own hut, but the smell was wrong and as she opened her eyes noticed the markings on the pelts were of no animal she could recognize. A light rap on the door brought her to full consciousness, and a thin pale boy, his skin almost luminescent, entered carrying a silver tray on which rested a stone mug and some fruit in a wooden bowl. Naldi smiled at the boy and he smiled back shyly as he placed the tray on the floor beside the bed, turned, and then exited the room.

Naldi was ravenously hungry. She picked up one of the seven different pieces of foreign looking fruit and held it to her nose. The size and shape of a pear, it smelled like a banana and was the color of a raspberry. As she bit into it, bright red juice ran between her fingers. *Absolutely delicious,* she thought, and as she took a second bite, her front teeth hit a small hard seed in the middle. She picked the dark seed out with her fingers and turning it to catch the light, admired the small heart shape of it. She ate the rest of the juicy sweet flesh, then took a small sip of water before choosing another piece of fruit. This second piece, about the size of a fist, was shaped like a five-pointed star. It smelled similar to the wild roses which grew in the meadows around her home. Naldi pulled it apart to see where the seed was and saw creamy white flesh dotted with tiny black specks she concluded must be the seeds. She bit into it and marveled at its succulent softness and delicate flavour.

As Naldi ate each piece of fruit in turn, she was invigorated by the natural sugars and enjoyed the scintillating sensation they left on her palate. The water had also refreshed her considerably but she still felt quite dehydrated. Taking the goatskin canteen which lay neatly amongst her other possessions on the stone floor, she drank a small quantity of the water from the river that ran past her home. Mixed emotions swirled within her as she thought of her friends and family. She had known it was unlikely she would return from her journey into the portal since only a few other *nag pa* ever had, but the sense of loss was still painful. Placing the canteen back on the floor she removed the large egg-shaped rock the other tribe had given her from her tapestry bag, and turning it in her hands thought of how kindly those people had treated her. "Why won't this woman let me go home?" she spoke to the pale light streaming in through the small window to her left, tears misting her vision. She lay back on the animal pelts and fell into a restless sleep.

Naldi was standing on the summit of the mountain overlooking the city below as one of two suns was cresting the horizon. The other sun was directly overhead but radiated only mild warmth. Naldi reeled in fear, an horrific screeching destroying the serenity she was feeling, as two huge birds swooped towards her. Her heart leapt into her throat and she froze, staring in disbelief as the two birds towering over her rapidly descended with their claws outstretched. She could smell their putrid breath as their wings beat the foul air down onto her. The larger of the two creatures sank its claws into her chest and back, and she woke with a scream.

Moments later, a woman about Naldi's age, dressed in a white toga cinched at the waist with a braided sliver cord, came into her room and sat down beside her, holding a cup of pungent smelling dark liquid. Raising the cup to her own lips she made the universal drinking motion and proffered it to Naldi. Naldi intuited that the brew was to calm her nerves, took a long sip and made a face of disgust as she swallowed. The girl smiled and encouraged Naldi to drink some more. "It's disgusting," said Naldi, and again the woman smiled but said nothing. "I know you can't understand me but I need to talk. Naldi is my name," she said pointing to herself and the woman understood.

The woman then spoke, pointing to herself also.

"Sheshun?" asked Naldi, approximating what she thought she heard, and the woman smiled brightly, nodding her head. Pointing to the empty platter, Naldi then rubbed her belly and said, "I am hungry." Sheshun handed the cup to Naldi and left the room while Naldi finished the bitter brew. She returned several minutes later with a small bowl of warm cooked grains topped with some sprouts. She held out a stubby wooden spoon, gave both objects to Naldi and took away the platter and cups. Naldi ate slowly and enjoyed the mildly salted food and refreshing sprouts. Finishing the gruel, she placed the bowl on the floor and walked to the window. Standing with her face in the pale sunlight she took several deep breaths. *How am I going to get home?*

Chapter One - Dreams May Come

Towering over a remote Nepalese village stands a mountain. If you ask any of the old farmers what is special about this particular mountain, pointing, they will tell you, through a sparse array of yellowing teeth and in the singsong broken English they have acquired of late, 'abode of the Gods'. The mountain isn't special in appearance, and to the many tourists who have now traveled to the region, looks spectacularly familiar to the rest of the mountains in this part of the world. But of course, there is a reason why they come.

Before Shala had even heard of the Portal of Creation, it had been appearing in her dreams. She was describing her latest dream to Angie, her newest best friend, as they both sat drinking chai lattes in a café downtown, the warm spring sunshine misting the morning dew like curlicues of smoke rising from the tips of a thousand lit cigarettes.

"I was standing on the side of a mountain looking down into the valley below, watching bright moonlight sparkle off the river meandering past a small village. Behind me was an immense presence. The energy was intense, but neither frightening nor benevolent."

"Do you remember what you were wearing?" asked Angie after taking a sip on her latte.

"Not exactly. I think I came from the village below and was dressed in whatever it was that a local woman would wear."

"Then what happened?" inquired Angie, no hint of the jealousy she felt whenever Shala spoke of her dream life. *My dreams are so boring*, she thought as she distractedly glanced to the nearest table where a cute guy in a well-cut suit had just taken a seat. She could smell his cologne and approved; the spicy sweet smell of Opium by Yves Saint Laurent. She thought of Philipe. *Hmm, holiday flings are fun.*

"Sorry, what did you say?" asked Angie.

"As I turned towards the mountain it felt as though my heart was going to burst. Well, not heart, more like my heart Chakra." Angie knew that was coming. *Oh my God*, she whispered under her breath as Shala closed her eyes and took a long meditative draught of her creamy sweet tea.

Shala and Angie met at a Chakra Healing workshop facilitated by one of Shala's inner circle of friends. Angie happened to see it advertised in the back of the local weekly street mag. Always looking for new opportunities in the self-development movement, it was Angie's desire to experience a more spiritual connection to the world around her. However, her real experiences of the workshops involved hearing story after amazing story recounted by the other participants. Sometimes, during the sharing circle at the end of the sessions, Angie would simply make stuff up. It was very easy to put together a two minute synopsis of other people's experiences from previous workshops. It's not that Angie didn't feel great from attending, but she never saw Ascended Masters, met her Spirit Guides, felt the electric tingle of Kundalini, heard Celestial music, went Astral traveling, or any other of the countless wonders recounted by her fellow participants.

"So what did you do?" asked Angie pointedly, jolting Shala out of her reverie.

"Pardon? Oh, nothing. I woke up. But I've had the same dream the last three nights."

"Do you think you will be able to get past your fears?"

"What do you mean?" asked Shala, her steely gaze, poised like an axe ready to bite in the heart of a dry winter forest, sending a chill down Angie's spine.

"Well, it seems to me as though there is something important for you to discover by entering into the presence you described," replied Angie, only slightly nervously. She had already worked out in their short relationship that pissing off Shala was a mistake. However, she was no pushover either.

"I don't think it's *my* fear that wakes me. I think it's the native woman. She knows what happens or has heard stories from her tribe. It's her trepidation I feel."

"Oh, I thought you said your heart Chakra felt like it would burst" replied Angie, who loved playing the devil's advocate. Shala put down her mug, picked up a recycled paper napkin, made from previously recycled paper, and dabbed around her exquisitely shaped mouth. "Dreams are complex Angie, you know that." Putting the napkin into her hand-woven handbag, the one she bought from the long-neck women in the highlands of Laos, so as not to waste the paper, Shala continued, "I think she is me from a past life."

The New-Age movement's winning coup de tat - the past life experience. Who could argue? Why would you bother, it only made you look like a nonbeliever.

"Oh, I get it. Of course, that makes sense," Angie replied through gritted teeth. All the while thinking - *so pretentious. Why are they certain there are such things as past lives? There are many ways to interpret transpersonal experiences but it seems no one is willing to discuss it anymore. More people need to read the transpersonal cartography of Dr. Stanislav Grof!*

"Hey, let's go check out the ice breaking up at the river," said Shala, as she pushed back her chair and picked up her bag, a thin line of milky froth still clinging to the tiny hairs above her naturally ruddy cupids bow, akin to Clark Gable's debonair mustache.

Frankly, I don't give a damn! "Sorry, can't. I have a doctor's appointment," lied Angie.

"Nothing serious, I hope?" asked Shala, an expression of deep concern having accosted her face. Her dark eyes showing genuine condolence.

"No, no, just a ruptured appendix, I'll be alright," quipped Angie, enjoying the momentary gullibility Shala would express.

"LOL. You're funny Angie. Hugs!" A brief embrace and Shala was off on her new adventure. Angie went home wishing she could be as in the moment as Shala.

Sitting in her kitchen, her cat Regression on her lap, Angie logged-on to facebook and scrolled through the latest entries from her network of friends.

Angie is an attractive, intelligent girl, but thinks her friends are far more interesting than her. She is highly sensitive. She has elfin features; a small upturned nose, little ears and large green compassionate eyes. Her jaw is strong, signaling a defiant will when needed. Her hair is shoulder length and dark brown with a hint of red, which she has highlighted through dyeing on numerous occasions.

Angie is a modern girl, and very progressive in her views on life. Unfortunately she has a tendency to confuse ideals with reality, and is often disappointed with her friends and family, and especially her partners. She has been with a handful of men, and tends towards falling in love with her sexual partners as she yearns to connect more deeply, striving to achieve pure and refined experiences of intimacy. This however, combined with the realities of day-to-day living, and layers of baggage yet to be shed, is an oftentimes illusive goal. Regardless, her mantra is to love deeply, and although she does experience moments of blissful-connectedness, it often results in heartbreak.

Her current boyfriend Archer, is handsome, intelligent and witty. They enjoy each other's company greatly. Egotism, however, overtakes him at times which translates into a lack of sensitivity to the subtler aspects of what she feels are essential to a healthy relationship. She often questions whether her needs are being met, or whether her expectations are simply too high. Angie added two friends to her friend-list on facebook. She met them both while participating in a hoola-hoop workshop at a festival the previous weekend. The festivals always bring out the best in people and Angie loves to dance.

Angie then clicked on Shala's profile to see what this weekend would have in store. Several dance parties, a yogalates workshop and an art exhibition. "Same old, same old," she said to Regression, as she scratched under his chin.

Angie clicked on the attending button for each of the events Shala was going to and thought of calling her boyfriend Archer. "Nothing like a roll in the hay to lift a girl's spirits," she said pressing her nose up to Regression's. "Feeling just a little manic today, my flabby fluff ball of love. Arghhhh," she growled as she wrestled him to the floor. The big tabby managed to work his way out of her grip and Angie was left lying on the floor, pouting and with a tear in her eye. *"Why am I so emotional?"*

She stood up, closed her laptop and went and lay on her bed. Looking through the titles on the pile of books on her bedside table, she sighed, curled into fetal position and closed her eyes.

Shala was again standing on the mountainside and behind her the same intense energy was urging her to turn around. She spoke aloud into the breeze billowing wisps of her long dark hair, and heard words she didn't understand. Shala's perspective changed as she realized it wasn't her that spoke, and looking down from beyond the edge of the mountain, watched as the woman turned and disappeared into the rock face. She awoke to the gentle rocking of her partner Trevor.

"You were making that sound again," he said as she opened her eyes; consciousness rushing in.

"Oh, sorry honey," cooed Shala, "I was back on the mountainside. The woman said, *'pukhār rakchyaa bããcnu'*, I'll have to write it down and look it up in the morning. As she spoke those words, I was shot out of her body and hovered nearby, while she turned and walked into the mountain. The strange thing was it all looked like solid rock from where I was. I need to stay connected and see if I can travel with her. I think this could be a huge step for me."

"Goodnight sweetheart. Turn the light out when you're done," said Trevor sleepily, as he kissed Shala on the cheek and rolled over. Smiling, Shala placed pen to paper and wrote phonetically the phrase she had heard the woman utter to the wind.

Shala had been keeping a dream diary for several years and was extremely appreciative of Trevor and his patience. Moreover, she was indebted to the fact that he was a light sleeper and would wake her whenever she would make that sound. Although Shala had never heard the sound, Trevor had tried to imitate it for her. *Similar to a strangled banshee*, she mused. *Poor Trevor.* Shala had worked on a way to wake herself from the dream state and that eerie sound was her triumph.

She read over a couple of the latest entries from her dreamscape upon that lonely mountainside. '*As I stand here, in simple tribal clothes, stone-bead bracelets on my arms, silver rings on my fingers, it seems as though my karma has placed me here. I am nervous but not scared. Quietly anticipating a wondrous journey. I feel privileged, but I (Shala) don't know why.* And another, *Looking down on her little village by the river, I sense her wondering if she will ever return. Thoughts, stories, images, flash upon my mind's eye. Campfire settings and tribal rituals - am I the Shaman's daughter?'*

Man that sounds schizophrenic, thought Shala. *I wish it was a past life, then I could get some regression therapy and find out where I went. It's going to be difficult staying with her as she disappears into the mountainside. Okay, back to sleep.*

Shala never had a reoccurring dream twice in one night, although she did have 'serial dreams', as she liked to call them. Those dreams where it doesn't matter how many times you wake from them, as soon as you're asleep again, you pick up from where you left off.

"If only this dream could be like that. Oh well, at this rate, I will be back there again tomorrow night," she said before turning off the light. Shala then fell into R.E.M. sleep cycles until Trevor woke her getting out of bed to the sound of his annoying alarm. *Trevor's revenge*, she thought, as she dragged herself to the toilet.

    Angie decided she wasn't going to attend the Friday night dance party and would instead do an early Saturday morning Mysore yoga session and then head to the library and get some quality books to read. The pile of books beside her bed, which she had no interest in reading, evidenced the mood she had been in the last time she visited the library. *Too much self-help crap*, she thought. *Yes, I'm from Venus, yes, I love too much, yes, I have ten things – and a thousand more – I want to change about myself. Damn it! I just want to enjoy my life. Everybody seems so serious these days. Problems everywhere. Poverty, starving children, environment going to hell, corporate greed, government B.S... Arghhh! What happened to the carefree days of my youth? ...Who am I kidding, being a teenager wasn't all that great either... Damn it, I'm almost twenty-eight ...I need to go traveling and have an adventure... I need to make a list of where I want to go. How long? Glad I don't have too much holding me down...*

    Yep. I need an adventure. I wonder what Archer will say. Probably flip out, no doubt. What if he says he wants to come along? Nope. I need to go by myself. Where to go? India? Cambodia? Thailand? Vietnam? Asia somewhere for sure... Can't afford Europe. Peru? Brazil? Mexico? I'd like to study more of the Mayan culture and get a better understanding of 2012. I definitely don't believe in all the doom and gloom, but many of the transformation rants sound even more ludicrous. Man, it's hard to find good information these days. We live in the information overload age I reckon!

Asia by myself? Hmmm...Could just do the ashram stint in India to start. Meet some like-minded people, relax a bit. What is it I really want? Oh no, not that old chestnut again. Maybe Costa Rica, hang out by the beach, relax and read books, do nothing for six months? Probably go out of my mind with boredom. No self-discipline... Ashram somewhere sounds good. A bit of structure, not too expensive, if I find the right one.

Angie opened her eyes and uncrossed her legs. "And that's what we call meditation, don't we Reggie?" Regression took no notice of Angie as he sat contentedly on top of the lounge. "Sorry buddy, but I think you're off to the parent's for a while. You like it there anyway, they feed you way too much." Regression opened his eyes to thin slits and stared at Angie with the kind of disinterest only a cat can muster. "Yes, held in contempt, aren't I? You old sourpuss!"

"Oh well, that's what the midweek meditation will give you. A completely life-changing experience. Saturday, after yoga, I'm off to the library to borrow some books on traveling."

Angie got up and made sure Regression had some water and a little food in case he got hungry during the night; which he invariably did. Then she checked to make sure the doors were locked, brushed her teeth, and got into bed. *School finishes in six weeks. I guess I give them notice I'm not coming back next year. Am I really going to do this? Feels like it. Oh, it is exciting to have something to look forward to.*

With that as her final thought, she drifted off into a peaceful sleep and dreamt of exotic locations, sunshine, warm sandy beaches and attractive tanned men.

After the best Mysore yoga session Angie ever had, she headed to the library, extremely excited about her upcoming travel plans. Beside the library was the community hall and on a billboard out the front was advertised a seminar: '*Time - Real or Imaginary? A Journey Into The Heart of Physics.*' She glanced at her watch and made a mental note of the start time. She'd never heard of the scientist giving the lecture, but found the world of modern physics very intriguing.

After about two hours looking through books on Asia and South America, Angie still hadn't settled on a specific starting place for her journey. "I want to see it all," she muttered under her breath as she scanned several Lonely Planet books through the library's self-checkout.

She bought a chai latte, her new favourite morning beverage, from the cafe in the foyer of the community hall and made her way to a seat down the front. The audience was fairly large and made up of many grey-haired folk, men mostly, but a lot of women too. Looking around, she decided she was definitely the youngest person in attendance.

A woman she recognized from previous community events stood at the wooden podium tapping the top of a microphone to see if it was on. She welcomed everybody in the customary 'ladies and gentleman' fashion and introduced a man with a doctorate in nuclear physics. She went on to describe his career and achievements to date. "Dr. David

Opinski has spent countless hours collecting data and collating measurements of experiments done on the Large Hadron Collider in the Swiss Alps. He was part of the research team, measuring the microwave radiation purportedly left over from the Big Bang. Dr. Opinski also worked with the infamous Dr. Sergio Villanadrosyev" – chuckles from the audience, but Angie had no idea why – "on his theory of the electric universe. He will discuss why science will never discover gravitons, his theory on neutron stars, commonly referred to as quasars, holographic resonance of quantum electrodynamics and how entanglement works . He will then tie all this back to modern theories on time, membrane theory and the topology of fractal geometry, wormholes, and the role of consciousness and observation of the quantum field effect."

Oh, this should be good, thought Angie, as she tried to get a little less uncomfortable on the foldout metal chair. She looked around and noticed how many others had brought their own small pillows. *I wonder if I'll ever get that practical? Born of aching joints and muscles, no doubt. Yoga is my cure. I would rather be sitting in full lotus on the floor. Ha, that would turn some heads. Stupid uncomfortable chair.*

Just then, applause erupted as Dr. Opinski walked on stage and stood beside the lectern. *Wow, he's handsome. He looks like that James Bond actor from the nineties, what's his name... Damn, I'm bad with names!*

After the clapping had subsided and the woman had left the stage, David closed his eyes and began a short chant. *The Gayatri mantra,* gushed Angie and followed along almost inaudibly. By the end of the second cycle, she knew she had a crush on a man nearly twenty years her senior. *What a beautiful voice. Worldly. Smart. I wish Shala was here.*

"All of us are subconsciously in tune with the generative principle of the fabric of reality, the inherent design of the universe as a whole and recognize such beauty when faced with the forms of that natural law," he stated, his eyes still closed. "Beyond metaphors, residing in the space between idea and opinion is the realm of experiential phenomena, the world perceived through direct contact, uncontaminated by the artificial texturing of our language, beliefs and conditioning. Is it possible for an individual to experience the world directly and not perceive through the lens of cultural misrepresentation? I ask this, because of the immediate conflict which arises upon having experiences outside the cultural constructs of learned and accepted knowing. This realm is traditionally the playground of the insane." A broad grin spread upon Dr. Opinski's face as he opened his eyes; a cheeky sparkle lighting the room.

"Science, in its quest of discovery, denies the existence of the individual perceiver through an inability to allow the observer to participate in any qualifying capacity. There simply is no room for subjective interpretation in science. By pure logical extension science can never know the whole system if it cannot accept the role of subjective mind. Objectivity is the line in the sand over which science dares not step and thus becomes the barrier to piercing the mystery of existence. There will be no Theory of Everything if it does not include consciousness.

Transcendence of duality is the new science paradigm. Only one field of scientific inquiry deals with epistemological knowing in a unifying format and that is ontology. Ultimately all science branches from this one discipline; the department of metaphysics concerned with the essence of Being. Ontologists know the only valid technology, which can be applied for scientific inquiry, is the interface of the human mind and body". He moved around the small platform, a tiger in cat's pajamas. Angie was transfixed by the pure energy she could sense smoldering deep within him.

"Our sentient intelligence used according to its evolutionary mandate is to create a feedback loop, reiterating the experience of the fractal dimension of infinity." Looking directly at Angie he said, "If ever there was a purpose to Creation and any meaning implicit in the complexity of the human organism, I believe it is as a device through which the Universe can know itself."

Angie was thoroughly enchanted, and as Dr. Opinski broke eye contact she looked around the room and noticed everyone's rapped attention.

David continued. Every word he spoke heavy with the truth of his conviction. "A whole system by definition is one in which all duality has been put into perspective and recognized as aspects of a cohesive continuum. The synthesis of consciousness and morphology leads to an experience of this cohesive whole. There is no difference between what we label spiritual and what we label physical. Metaphysics understands this unity. This includes subjective and objective mind and its relation to time-space. Every observer has their own relative and therefore subjective experience. An ontologist uses his or her own mind-body as the scientific apparatus in the experiment to find an answer to the question 'what is the true nature of being?'. Acknowledging the positive feedback loop created between the observer and the observed when this delineation is dissolved, the ontologist becomes a boundless self-referential singularity spread across all space".

Angie appreciated that David spoke slowly and eloquently. However, his words came from a place of deep connection to something Angie couldn't fathom. "As a self-aware occupier of hyperspace - a singularity - all the complexities of existence are experienced as a divergence from the simple space of the unformed, as no aspect of self can be excluded from the whole. All meaning arises from the fact that there exists an organism as complex as the human in context to a much vaster system. It is our sentient intelligence which creates meaning out of the pure pattern of complex form. Fortunately for us, space being a vibrating fractal continuum, we resonate as a microcosm of the macrocosm".

David paused for a moment, took a sip of water and then quoted Martin Rees the famous astrophysicist. "In the beginning there were only probabilities. The universe could only come into existence if someone observed it. It does not matter that the observers turned up several billion years later. The universe exists because we are aware of it."

With arms outstretched he continued. "We exist in a universe in which individual brains are indivisible portions of the macrocosm and everything is infinitely interconnected. Our senses measure the wavelengths to which they are tuned and from which the body is formed. Built of the same wavelengths of electromagnetism that comprise all structures in the measurable universe, holographically we contain and are made of all the information of the whole system. If the concreteness of the world is but a vibrating continuum, and if our brain measures these frequencies and mathematically transforms them into sensory perceptions, what becomes of objective reality? In a holographic universe there are no limits to the way in which we may participate in shaping reality!"

David spent the next hour and a half speaking about many theories that went against nearly everything Angie thought she knew about the world in which she lived. She couldn't conceptualize what kind of question she could possibly ask. *I need to buy his book.* 'The Fractal Edge of Universal Mind - The Jewel Glittering in Hyperspace' - *quite the title*, she thought as she approached the book-signing table, a hardcover copy in her hand. *Very generous of them to give everyone a free book. I guess he's not in desperate need of the money.* Then she noticed it. In the bottom left hand corner of the book, a golden sticker in the shape of a disc and the words 'Over One Million Sold' embossed around the circumference. "Whoa!" she exclaimed, and the woman in front of her turned with a quizzical expression on her face. "Sorry. I had no idea," she said pointing to the decal.

"Do you live in a cave?" said the woman, not unkindly.

"Pretty much," replied Angie, not the least perturbed.

David looked up from the opened copy of Angie's book and enquired to whom he should address the signing.

"Angie." She blurted, her excitement from noting the pleasing look upon David's face as he looked up at her. She blushed and looked down as he wrote: *'To Angie, may your journey be as beautiful as your smile'*, followed by the flourish of someone who has signed their name more times then Angie had probably brushed her teeth. "Are you in town long?" She asked before she knew what she had said.

"Unfortunately not this trip, but I will be back in two weeks for another lecture. A private function for some" he looked around conspiratorially "dignitaries." He wrote something quickly on a piece of paper as he said this, slipped it into her book, closed it and handed it back. The twinkle in his eyes was unmistakable. *He's way younger up close.* She smiled, blushed and moved out of the way.

Making her way to the exit, she opened the book and there on the tiny piece of paper was his cell phone number. She reread the note he had written. The cynical Angie kicked into gear. *I wonder how many times he's written that? Probably the stock message for every woman under forty, but he's handsome and he's smart. So glad Shala wasn't here. Damn my insecurities.* She conjured up the image of his twinkling brown eyes, as she made her way back to her car. *I'm sure he liked me. He did look at me several times during his lecture too. Wow, I'm such an idiot. Of course he knew I was planning a journey*, she realised as she placed the other three books she was carrying onto the roof of her car and retrieved her keys from her handbag. *Man, such easy prey, a woman with desires*, she mused as she got behind the wheel of her car. *One thing is for sure; I am not going to call him.* "He's like a rock-star for geriatrics," she said out loud to affirm the sentiment.

She wound her way through the car park and headed for home. Instead of taking a right into her neighbourhood, she kept going straight. "I want to see the ice breaking-up down at the river," she said, again out loud to affirm her convictions. She caught herself, "Nothing quite like making a statement and being able to execute it for immediate reward. I am a powerful being!" she sang the last sentence jokingly.

Angie parked her car in the car park next to the river and grabbed the library books, then David's book only on second thought. She realized she was still quite annoyed at what a blushing idiot she had been at the book-signing table. *But he is so smart*, she thought, as she made her way down to the river's edge. *I love this early spring weather. Too bad winter can drag on for so long.*

After about ten minutes of breaking glass-clear ice sheets underfoot and reveling in the crunching and tinkling sounds of the shattering ice, Angie squatted beside her pile of books. "I definitely like the look of you guys, better than that last lot," she said, with a bemused smile. As she tugged on the copy of Lonely Planet's Guide to India, which had been second from the bottom of the four books, she inadvertently sent David's book sliding down the bank of dry brown grass towards the river's edge. "Shit!" she screamed and leapt forward from her squat and dived to grab it before it got wet.

Sprawled belly down on the bank, 'India' in her left hand, and 'The Fractal Edge of Universal Mind' in her right, a lightning bolt of awareness exploded up from the base of her spine and she knew that somehow she had changed the fate of her life this day. "Oh, what have I done?"

She lay there, her eyes shifting from one book to the other, flashes of images dancing behind her open eyes. She closed them to see what was going on. Some of the images looked like television footage of documentaries on India. Interspersed with crowded market places, temples, colourful religious festivals and rivers and mountains, were inexplicably beautiful patterns. "Mosaics," she whispered. "No. More like ancient tapestries, or a thousand spiral galaxies. Snowflakes and sunflowers. Weird."

She opened her eyes, but still the images continued. Using her elbows she pushed herself awkwardly to her knees, turned around and placed the two books beside her. Kneeling now in the yoga posture Virasana, or hero's pose - her bottom resting on her heels with her toes pointing down hill - she again closed her eyes. Nothing. *That's weird.* She placed her hand on David's book and instantly her mind's eye was filled with patterns. "Mandalas. It looks like I'm standing in a forest, looking up through all the branches, or I'm looking down on a river system and its tributaries as seem from a satellite. This is so cool!"

She let go of David's book and placed her hand on the guide to Costa Rica and immediately she knew she was there. She saw images of lush rainforest and beautiful white sandy beaches dissolving into deep turquoise waters. *This is incredible.* She opened her eyes and looked around. With the images of Costa Rica still playing, she took her hand off the book and could see clearly her riverside surroundings.

Everything is so alive and scintillating. There seems to be a fabric "a mosaic, connecting everything" she whispered. *What are all these colours too? Purple, indigo and violet. So many shades of blue and orange and green and red.* Everywhere Angie looked she could see a vast network of interwoven swirling colours.

"Maybe I'm having a stroke!" She thought about Jill Bolt Taylor, the woman she had watched on Ted.com, giving a talk about her experience of having a stroke. Angie stood up slowly. "Hello, my name is Angela Crystal Winters. My cat's name is Regression," *nope, that all sounded normal. I think I'll call Shala just in case.* Angie pulled her cell phone from her bag and pressed the call history icon and clicked on Shala. The phone rang and almost immediately Shala's sleepy voice answered. "Hello."

"Sorry, did I wake you? What's the time?" Glancing at her phone "Oh, 12:35pm."

"Yeah, it was a big night. Didn't get in until 9:30 this morning" said the sleepy Shala.

"No problem. I'll call you later" Angie replied, too excited to care.

"Bye," was the reply from Shala as she hung up.

Good, thought Angie, *no stroke victim today it seems. It kind of reminds me of that LSD trip I took with Sarah and Renee all those years ago. Maybe someone slipped something into my latte when I was at the community center.* She thought back over her morning and was surprised at the level of detail she was able to recall from the morning's events.

"This is seriously weird!" said Angie as she pictured herself standing in the library, glancing at titles in the travel section and hearing a conversation happening two aisles away. A conversation she was certain she didn't even notice the first time. In her mind's eye, she saw herself turn her head and look to see if she could spy on who was talking. She saw them; a Chinese guy about her age chatting with one of the librarians. They were discussing the current clampdown by the Chinese government on access to information on the Internet, for the Chinese people.

Even though they were whispering, she could clearly hear every word. That wasn't the surprising thing. What she couldn't comprehend was how she could look at them now when she knew for certain she hadn't even glanced at them this morning. She opened her eyes. "Whoa!" she exclaimed as she looked up river. Still the colours whirled around. She decided to go to another moment from earlier in the morning. Dr. Opinski had just walked onto the little raised stage and stood beside the lectern.

Angie spent the next few minutes with her eyes closed, watching and listening to David give his talk. *I'm sure this is word for word.* The mantra, his opening dialogue, the little joke about wormholes and special relativity which she still didn't get. She jumped ahead to the book signing and found she could even pause the memory playback. "This is too cool! My own PVR on life." She froze the scene with David looking up at her, just after she had said her name. She watched, frame-by-frame it seemed, as his eyes dropped to the books clasped in her left hand, between her hip and waist, before they continued on to the inside cover of her book. *Yes, there it is. So subtle. Not even the slightest hesitation to compose the lines. Beautiful.*

Angie opened her eyes again and reveling in the swirling colours, noticed that her clothes, hands and legs were also part of this ecstatic dance. *I'm taking this home. Hope I can drive,* she thought slightly concerned, collecting the books and walking back to her car. Behind the wheel she took a few deep calming breaths. *An overblown stress response to almost losing David's book and his phone number? Possibly. I have been really stressed recently. Maybe this is the after effects of being so tightly wound?* Angie put the index finger and middle finger of her left hand up to her neck and measured her pulse rate. *About ninety beats per minute,* she concluded after fifteen-seconds. *Fairly normal considering. Well, I feel fine to drive. I'll go and have a nice warm bath with some lavender,* she decided as she started her car. Then she thought of Archer. *I wonder what sex would be like in this state of heightened awareness?*

She felt tingles around her lower belly and closed her eyes to see if she could bring more awareness to the area. There, in the lower part of her abdomen and pelvis, she saw two bright glowing orbs. The lower was a dark fiery red and the other a bright orange. *This is way cool! My chakras, I can see my chakras! I'm sitting in my car, the engine's running and my chakras are lit up like Christmas tree lights. OK. Need to get home.* Angie opened her eyes and focused all her attention on driving her car back to its resting place in the basement of her apartment building.

Once inside her home, she went straight to Regression and gave him a huge hug. "Oh, my little guy. Mommy has definitely lost it this time. I can see chakras. I can even see your little cat aura by the looks of it. Crazy, but there seems to be a soft luminescence around you." Regression was purring very loudly. "You like this, don't you! I'm on your wavelength now."

Angie left Regression in a state of cat bliss, crossed through the kitchen, walked down the hall and grabbed some clean towels from the closet before entering her bathroom and running a bath. She undressed and stood gazing into the full length mirror on the front of the shower door. Normally, Angie would avoid seeing herself naked. Vanity of course being one of the seven deadly sins. However, that wasn't really the reason. Nakedness had always made her feel uncomfortable. For as long as she could remember, she didn't like seeing anyone naked. She especially didn't like anyone seeing her naked. The girls' showers after gym practice had always been an anticipated time of not wanting to appear to be 'that girl' and being fully aware that she was 'that girl'. For a few years, Angie thought she may have a serious problem with her sexuality. "I'm just shy. I blame too much church indoctrination" she would chide herself. Later it was her boyfriends that made her feel awkward. *They were even worse! Bits and pieces flopping around everywhere. No modesty whatsoever and wanting me to lay around naked all the time too.*

This time she stood there looking at herself, minus the old thought patterns. "I am a beautiful woman," she stated, as though it was the honest to god truth. She pulled the hair band from out of her hair and brought all her hair forward through her fingers, to rest on her shoulders. "I am so beautiful," she said again, twisting from side to side. "I am perfect the way I am." She had said both these statements to the mirror many times in the past, but never with conviction.

"What in the world happened to me today?" she queried, as she turned off the running water, and added a few drops of lavender from the aromatherapy kit her sister Sophie gave her for Christmas several years ago. She thought of Sophie and how much she loved her. *"Ah, meine kleine schwester. You too are beautiful!"*

Stepping into the hot water, she remembered she wanted to call Archer and tell him to come over. Just as she stepped back out onto the bathroom rug, the phone rang. "Archer! Good timing buddy," she said as she strode for the cordless phone on the wall in the hallway outside the kitchen.

"Hello?"

"Hi Baby." It was Archer in a good mood.

"Hello gorgeous," said Angie in the huskiest voice she ever heard come from her mouth. "I'm naked," she drawled, before Archer even had time to respond.

"Are you okay?" asked Archer, genuinely concerned.

"Of course. Why shouldn't I be? I was just about to have a bath. You wanna come over?"

Archer knew something was different, but he liked what he heard. "Sure babe. What time?"

"Whenever you're ready." Came the heady reply. "I'm already wet!" Archer's phone made a clunking noise in Angie's earpiece.

"You okay, Arch?" asked Angie then smiled to herself as she walked back into the bathroom.

"Sure. Yeah. Just fumbled the phone. I'll be there in about forty-five minutes."

"I'll be waiting!" said Angie, as she lay the phone down on the sink and slithered into the warm fragrant water. She felt between her legs and parted her flower tenderly. "Oh my god. I'm so wet!" With her eyes closed, Angie watched mooladhara chakra with its fiery red glow spin faster and faster, burning brighter and brighter as she slowly brought herself to climax. She watched as wave after wave of what looked like ectoplasm shoot up her spine as she arched up out of the water. "Archer isn't going to know what hit him!"

David was sitting in first class on the domestic jet, nibbling his complimentary nut mix and marveling at how he couldn't take his mind off the gorgeous girl from the morning's lecture. *Angie. Wow. How old is she? Probably mid twenties. I wonder if she'll call. I can't believe I gave her my number.* He thought of his best friend Danny and his comment that he should have more fun.

"You're always hanging out with people your parent's age. You need to meet some girls. You know what they say, 'All work and no play'. You're only thirty-six, man, you need to party. Let your hair down!" David chuckled to himself. *At least I didn't ask for her number. That would have been bad in front of all those lovely people. But will she call? She no doubt has a boyfriend. Come to think of it, she probably thinks I give out my number to every attractive woman. Wish I could! Here I am, I've cracked the riddle of the universe but have no clue how to pick up women. She is different though. Genuine. In that brief moment, I fell into her very essence. The eyes truly are the windows to the soul.*

"Ready for takeoff." The flight attendant's words jolted him back into to the present. David looked up and saw the flight attendant smiling at him before she looked towards the back of the plane and continued down the aisle. It was then he noticed the big grin plastered across his face. *I'm falling in love with a girl I'll probably never see again.* Picking up a magazine from the pouch in front of him, he opened to an article on the wonders of Teotihuacan, and let Angie slip from his mind.

Chapter Two - Sleeper Awake

It was almost 6pm when Archer pressed the buzzer on the intercom to Angie's apartment. She had light an array of candles in her bedroom and put her ipod on to play a random selection of her favourite lounge music. Down tempo tunes, she had discovered, kept men from getting excited too fast. She wanted this evening's love making to be slow, soft and long. *This might be the closest I ever get to tantric sex,* she mused.

Angie buzzed Archer in and told him to come straight to the bedroom. Archer had no witty reply. The statement *'Don't come in unless you're naked'* had left him speechless. As Archer climbed the two flights of stairs to her floor, he noticed he was feeling a little intimidated. His male insecurities, usually so well hidden by his macho demeanour, were making him feel extremely self conscious. He entered her flat with the key she had given him, went to the fridge and poured himself a glass of orange juice. *I need something stronger,* he thought to himself, finishing the drink in one long pull. Looking through the fridge for something to snack on, he realized that he was quite unsure of what awaited him in the bedroom and whether he was really up to the task. Finding nothing besides a vast array of inexplicable condiments, he closed the fridge, took a few deep breaths and walked down the hall to stand outside Angie's door.

He thought of what a beautiful girl Angie was and started to undress. Her earlier comment reverberated in his mind. *Tonight is her night. Whatever she wants she gets.* Slowly pushing open the door, he saw the flickering light from candles and shadows dancing on the bedroom walls. Archer crept silently into the room, noticed Angie's eyes were closed, a beautiful soft smile lighting her face and stood there for a moment drinking in her sublime perfection and feeling the anticipation of what was to come.

Angie opened her eyes slightly and tilted her head a little to the opposite side. Archer recognized the cue. He moved slowly to the bed and, brushing the hair from around Angie's neck, began a series of little butterfly kisses up to her ear. She purred like a kitten in response, and rolled a little more to the side, giving Archer access to the sensitive areas below her hairline around the nape of her neck. Archer lifted the duvet and climbed in behind Angie, his manhood pressing into the small of her back. Angie reached her right hand down and taking hold of him, guided him into the fire between her legs. Archer heard the quietest of gasps escape Angie's pouting lips as he slowly entered her. He couldn't believe how soft and hot she felt. It took all his control not to come in that very instant.

Angie sensed the intensity of Archer's need to focus on suppressing his orgasm. She didn't move a muscle and simply enjoyed the pulsing sensation. *This is so incredible*, she thought, as she focused her mind's eye into the area where they were joined. Angie could see the same ectoplasmic light emanating from Archer's penis, thought of Luke Skywalker's light saber, and let out a small giggle.

"What's so amusing?" asked Archer, barely able to keep it together, but thankful for the distraction.

"Oh nothing, my little Jedi Knight," quipped Angie, "just make sure you're feeling the Force."

Archer closed his eyes too and felt Angie's wetness, like silk flowing over his loins. He felt Angie reach between his legs, lightly massage his testes and pull them gently away from his body, which they both knew greatly reduced his desire to ejaculate.

Once Angie was satisfied that Archer wasn't going to come, she again focused her attention into the core of her being and took the shaft of intense electrical light, and used it to stir the molten pot of liquid ecstasy pooling there. *I've read enough to know what's going on,* she thought as little sparks started to arc up from within. Moving her hips in an undulating rhythm to the pulses of electrical discharge, she increased their frequency and amplitude. She felt pins and needles in her feet and, taking her awareness there, released the small crystal-like blockages she could see preventing more liquid light energy from entering through her soles.

Curling and uncurling her toes helped open up the afferent pathways. *Meridians. Chi!* With this realization it was as though floodgates had been opened and the electrical plasma energy coursed up her legs to merge with the already intense pool of fiery liquid light at her core. She let out a loud moan of primal pleasure. The hairs on the back of Archer's neck stood up sending shivers cascading down his back and thighs.

Angie moved her awareness up along her spine and saw each of her chakras in succession. Each of the spinning vortexes of energy above the root chakra were beginning to get brighter too. Angie watched with the eye of inner seeing, as the twin male and female energies Ida and Pingala, snaked their way around Sushumna the vertical etheric column along her spine.

As the serpent energy excited Manipura, Anahata, Vishudi and Ajna chakras, memories came flooding into her mind. Not only memories from her current lifetime; joyous memories of time spent with family and friends, sublime moments of incredible joy and pure love, but also memories of other incarnations. All the images were moments where great feelings of love had flowed naturally within her. As each chakra lit up increasingly, her senses were also further heightened. There was an audible click in her ears and suddenly she could hear the subtlest of sounds; all the auditory emanations in her apartment. She could hear Archer's quiet rhythmic breathing as he held on for the ride of his life. She could hear the sound of the candles as their wicks were being consumed by the mysterious energy called fire. She could hear the quiet hum of the electrical grid running throughout her home, and off in his favourite spot on the couch in the lounge-room, she could hear Regression purring.

Her sense of touch, the whole kinesthetic stimulus from her organ of skin, was almost overwhelming. It seemed as though every square millimeter of flesh was sending a thousand shards of bliss to her brain. She inhaled deeply and rode a huge wave of ecstasy to a new level of awareness. As she exhaled, she heard the most primal, guttural sound she could imagine and realized it had come from her. *I am a biological being of light dancing in the void of infinite blackness*, was the thought that accompanied the sound. *Biology is a dance of light.* Waves of pleasure and bliss were crashing on the shores of her mind, and the horizon of her awareness was expanding. Focusing her attention within,

Angie saw galaxies colliding in a slow dance of destruction and creation. A play of incredible forces of which she was a part. *No, not a part. This is all me! I am this universal dance of creation and destruction. Form is temporary but energy is conscious and eternal.*

Like a key turning in a lock at the top of her head, there was an explosion of pure white light. *Now this is what I call the big bang,* she laughed to herself, as her mind rippled outwards into infinite space. *I am the beginning, middle and end. I am all space, seen and unseen. I am a being of pure consciousness beyond all duality. I am the universe experiencing itself!* Angie road waves of never-ending bliss as the universe poured out its secrets to her. She connected her consciousness to the entire family of consciousness. All beings in all dimensions of space and time were merged and expressing their love and compassion within her. She spiraled back through billions of years of evolution and felt the kinship of all creatures on Earth. Her mind flowed out around the planet and everyone was happy, everyone was rejoicing. Enemies were hugging, history had ended, there was no need for enmity as love was now the only experience. All karma had been dissolved.

I am all the creation myths made manifest! She saw all the great cultures of past and present. She understood their striving for contact with the Eternal, understood the purpose of the pyramids scattered all over the planet and all the other magnificent monuments dedicated to the quest of knowing. *This moment is all there is,* she knew in every molecule of her being. *I am the fractal edge of universal mind!* After this realization, there was bliss and an endless sea of pure love and she was floating on it for eternity.

Angie woke to the smell of freshly brewed coffee. She rolled over and looked at her clock. 9:47. *Maybe we can go to that dance party tonight. I feel amazing.*

Archer came into the room and placed a tray with two cups of coffee, a bowl of strawberries, a cup of honey yoghurt, and some flowers arranged in her small crystal vase onto the bed, walked over to the balcony doors and drew back the heavy chocolate-brown draperies. Sunlight poured in through the glass and she had to close her eyes and turn her head away.

"What in the world?" asked a very confused Angie.

"Oh, sorry honey, it's Sunday morning."

"What happened? Wow. I guess I must have passed out?"

"I know. I woke up about twenty minutes ago, still inside you. We hadn't moved from that position since I climbed into your bed around six o'clock last night. That was the most amazing sex I have ever had!" replied Archer, eyes wide and sparkling.

"You're telling me!" laughed Angie. "Oh my God. I will need to write down what happened," she said, as she dipped a strawberry into the honey yoghurt and popped it into her mouth. The explosion of flavour caught her unaware and she gasped and almost choked. Coughing she said, "Holy molly, these are tasty strawberries!" She closed her eyes and watched her taste buds send little electrical sparks up into her brain. *I wonder if this is ever going to go away? I hope not. If this is what it's like to be truly alive, I'm down!* She opened her eyes and looked at Archer as he sat there on the end of her bed gazing at her quizzically from over the top of his raised coffee mug.

"You wanna play some more, sweetheart?" she asked, before popping another strawberry into her mouth.

"Sure," he responded, only the slightest hint of trepidation in his voice.

Hearing a muffled wail, Trevor promptly woke Shala from her slumber. Coming into wakefulness, Shala burst into tears. "I just can't stay connected to her after she asks her ancestors to protect her. That's the fourth night in a row."

"Maybe she is going to her death and it wouldn't be safe for you to stay connected?" said Trevor, as he lay his hand on Shala's forearm. Trevor was an open-minded guy, but he had some difficulty relating to Shala's experiences. What he really wanted to say was "It's only a dream, get over it and go back to sleep. I have work in the morning." Trevor liked Shala a lot, and of course no friendship or relationship of most any kind can be shared with the truth of one's convictions and feelings being expressed so harshly. For Trevor, the human potential movement was hamstrung for this very reason. Nobody could *really* share their truth.

Trevor had been in numerous ceremonial circles over the past few years of his relationship with Shala and had heard plenty of people struggle trying to speak their truth and knowing that if they did, it would probably mean a shunning from the community for a while. Thankfully, because people are nervous when trying to work out what they can say when it's their turn, much of the essence of people's truth is hidden behind the word "like". The truth becomes a simile.

"It's as though I'm forced to wait. But for what?" said Shala.

"Or Who?" said Trevor, somewhat distractedly, as he was reminiscing on the half-truths he had spoken at so many closing circles.

"What do you mean, 'or who'?" asked Shala, turning to face Trevor, the tears evaporating away.

"Um. I don't know. Have you tried waiting to see if she steps back out from the cave or whatever it is? "

"Nice recovery," said Shala, liking the idea. "Maybe I will try that tomorrow night."

"Have you been shown any new information in the last couple of nights?" Asked Trevor, now fully awake. *Nothing quite like the steely gaze of Shala to bring you to your senses*, he thought.

"No. Nothing of any importance. Just more details coming into view. Her clothes, footwear, some stone bracelets. It's certainly a big moment for this woman. After reviewing more of her memories as she stands there looking down on her village, I am positive she is either the Shaman's daughter or the clan leader's daughter. Of course, the clan leader could be the Shaman. Either way, she is the chosen one for her generation. I also feel this practice has gone on for many generations."

"Is it a sacrifice?" asked Trevor, after glancing at his bedside clock and knowing there was no point trying to get back to sleep.

"No. Well, maybe. Not in the traditional sense. I feel the tribe is waiting for the time when one of the chosen ones is able to return from wherever it is they go when they enter the mountain. I feel the greatest sense of loss as she looks down on her village. She's certain she will never see it again."

"Sounds like a sacrifice to me!" said Trevor, being cautious not to be too dismissive.

"I guess so," responded Shala, as her eyes glazed over in the melancholy of her introspection. Then the tears came in earnest. Wracking sobs from deep within. "I want...to...find...that vill.....age."

Angie hadn't really come down from her Kundalini awakening but the intensity had subsided considerably, which was a great relief. Her first week back at school, however, was almost unbearable. The noise of the children, the emotional roller-coaster ride all teachers go on as the year ends, even little things like the smell of the student's lunches, were intense. During that first week, Angie found herself disappearing into the staff toilets for five minute snatches of quietude. *I just want to be at home meditating*, she would lament, as she sat on the toilet, her head in her hands, reminiscent of the mornings after a big night out: head spinning, nausea, sweats. *Quite the carnival ride. The only thing missing is the haunting melody of psychotic clown music.*

By the Friday of the first week Angie was exhausted. She went home, unplugged the phone and went straight to bed. The only food she could stomach were bananas and the only beverage that wouldn't come straight back up, was filtered water with a spritz of lemon juice. She had lost just over five pounds when she'd weighed herself Thursday night, and despite the tough week she could feel the power deep within which she was longing to reconnect to. "A good night's sleep and no partying this weekend should do it. Tomorrow some light yoga and a long yoga nidra session and I will be tiptop again," she whispered to the darkness of her bedroom, before rolling onto her side and falling into a deep, restful sleep.

Angie woke to a heavy feeling in her chest and scared herself in the fraction of a second before she realized Reggie was sleeping there. "You freaked me out, you lump!" she exclaimed, as she brought her right arm out from underneath her duvet and scratched Regression under his chin.

"Wow, what a sleep. I feel so much better." Glancing at her clock, "7:30. Awesome! That was about twelve hours my little Buddy. Mommy feels much better. Man, what a week!" Pulling herself into a sitting position she forced Reggie off her chest. He stood, turned around and moved into a luxurious stretch through several yoga asanas. "So easy for you, isn't it?" said Angie, as she pushed him onto his side. "Well, *my* turn now," she said, as she slipped out from under the covers and picked up her yoga pants and top from off the wooden chest at the end of her bed.

"Hungry Buddy?" she called over her shoulder, as she walked to the fridge and poured herself a glass of water and squeezed the juice of half a lemon into it. Peering through to the sunroom, she could see Reggie's bowl of water was full but that he barely had enough dry food for his breakfast. "Might have to put you on the fruit and water diet. You're the one who could lose a few pounds, my little lump of lovely lard!"

Taking a few sips of the mildly bitter liquid, she made her way into the spare bedroom and hit the power button on her ipod, found her favourite yoga playlist then stood at the top of her mat, eyes closed sipping her water.

Placing the empty glass to the side of her mat, Angie stood in Tadasana, hands together in Anjali mudra and focused her awareness on restricting moola bandha. Sensing the slight constriction around her perineum and up to her lower transverse abdominus, she saw a pillar of light rising up from the core of her being. With her mind's eye, she followed the growing spire as it made its way up her spine. She let it pass the spot where previously she would have activated uddhiyana bandha and let it continue to her throat where she felt compelled to activate jalandhara bandha and contain the growing pillar of luminescence. Once the upward flow had been stemmed, the column of light started to grow brighter and expand. It travelled along fine filaments, the light staying within the well defined network of nerves much the same way electrons are described flowing within copper wire.

Angie's breathing was slow, relaxed and steady, neither too deep, nor too shallow. Her mind felt clear. *No thought,* she thought, then caught herself. *Just breathe!* Focusing again on the visual light show within, Angie felt her whole body relax and rejuvenate as the prana bathed her body in its healing power. Angie continued with the inner gaze and watched as the electric blue-white light made its way into every cell in her body. The feeling was exquisite and Angie let the waves of pleasure wash over her, as all her subconscious fears and concerns melted away.

After several minutes of this exquisite pranic bath, she lifted her eyelids ever so slightly and could see little sparks of light dancing in the room around her. *So beautiful!* The sound of her internal dialogue physically jolted her, comparatively loud in her inner silence. *Crystal clear. Divine being. Life is pure magic.* These thoughts dissipated, becoming more like feelings now, than the word noise of mentality. *Effortless ebb and flow. Pure cosmic radiance. Eternal mind.* Angie lifted her hands above her head in tune with her inhalation and bent forward from her hips as she slowly exhaled. She moved through the entire primary series of asanas as if she had been practicing yoga for a thousand years.

As she lay back in savasana, at the end of her physical practice, she released the bandhas and rode the prana as a wave of pure love into the cosmic ocean. *I am one. All is me.* Floating in the stillness of being, Angie was at peace.

Time to plant my sankalpa, she thought, as she started the rotation of consciousness for her yoga nidra practice, moving her mind slowly from one body part to another. *This is definitely the deepest I have been into my subconscious. What wisdom or guidance do you have for me? Instruct me, what is my mission? What is my prime directive?* She smiled, thinking of Eva from the movie Wall-E. *I want to share my experiences. I want people to learn how to awaken their Kundalini and activate their chakras. Problem is, I'm not sure how I did. I had a spontaneous awakening.* She thought back to the previous Saturday. *Oh my god, that was only one week ago! People are going to think I'm crazy if I start talking about these experiences.* She pictured the look on Archer's face as he was leaving her place last Sunday. *Talk about taming a lion,* she mused. *What a doe-eyed look of gratitude and fear. Okay, sidetracked. What is my resolve? Do I share this or keep it secret? I need to develop my abilities some more and see where this inner knowledge can take me. Got it! My resolve is to keep exploring my new gifts.* Focusing all her attention onto the feeling of her intention, she let the sensation, the desire to explore the inner realms of power, compassion and wisdom, soak into every cell in her body.

David had spent that following weekend at two speaking engagements catching himself several times, scanning the faces of the audience for Angie. Sitting now in his hotel room, a scientific journal in his hands, the lines of text blurred as he stared through the pages into an imaginary scene beyond. Angie was walking towards him, her beautiful green eyes igniting within him a feeling of deepest passion and large crystals at her throat and third eye were throwing off reflections of rainbow light mesmerizing him. *She reminds me of an Atlantean Priestess.* She was wearing a pale green silk dress which willowed gently as she approached. *They aren't crystals, they are pure light - her chakras! She is so beautiful! I have fallen completely in love with you.* Angie stood in front of him, holding each of his hands in hers and he could feel their warmth. He breathed in deeply while Angie, standing on tippy-toes, kissed him gently on each cheek. A huge wave of sadness swept over him as she let go of his hands, turned and walked away.

David came out of his reverie, sighed, looked out his window and across the bay to a group of tiny sails illuminated by the mid morning sun. *I have all the success and money any bachelor could want and the one thing I can't have is all I can think about. Wait, facebook!* He put down the periodical and picked up his laptop. *Damn. I don't know her last name.* David typed "Angie" into the search field and thousands of results appeared. He then narrowed the search by adding the name of the town they had met. That reduced the number to just over five hundred. He started scrolling and soon realized the futility of his search. *Maybe I could call the library next to the community hall. She's obviously a member.* He typed the name of the community he had visited into the search engine, and then stopped. *What am I now, a stalker? I'm just going to have to wait until she calls me.* He closed his eyes, relaxed, and conjured up an image of her face. *Angie, I love you. Please call. You are all I think about. I am too old for a schoolboy crush. There is something very special about you.*

He opened his eyes after a few minutes of focused intention. *Nothing like putting your own theories to the test,* he thought, as he put down the laptop, stood up, and headed to the kitchenette to make himself a cup of tea.

Shala phoned Angie for the third time in as many days and again got her answering machine. "Hey Angie, it's Shala. It's Sunday afternoon. Please give me a call when you get this. I have some exciting news. Hugs." Shala hung up the phone, picked up her dream diary off her Balinese bedside table, walked out to the lounge room and sat cross-legged on the couch bathed orange in the fading afternoon sunlight.

Opening the diary to her last entry, she re-read words written in the wee hours of the previous morning. '*After again being knocked out of the native girl's experience and watching her enter what now looks definitely like an opening into a small cave, I am shot out into space and in the blink of an eye find myself looking down at the Earth. Instead of seeing land and water, I see geometric shapes and a vast network of intersecting lines.*

The place in the mountains where the native woman has disappeared is revealed as one of the vertices of a giant merkaba; two huge tetrahedrons nested in the shape of a three dimensional star of David, its eight points illuminated as giant vortices of writhing, swirling cosmic energy. From these points, I see fine electrical looking filaments wrapping around the globe in a lattice or giant spider web. The word songlines *springs to mind, and I hear the psychic radiation of a thousand generations of native cultures communing with the intelligence of the Earth.'*

Closing her eyes, Shala pictured what she could recall from the dream. *A planetary merkaba! Sweet revelation,* a smile spreading across her face. Getting up from the couch, she walked over to the bookshelf and pulled out *Sacred Geometry - The Language of Ascension* and flicked through the book from back to front. *Merkaba - divine light vehicle. Used by adepts to enter into realms of higher consciousness. Mer = light, Ka = spirit, Ba = body.*

Grabbing her oversized Atlas of the World from off the coffee table, she opened it to the mercator projection of the Earth, spread over the centre pages and following the latitude lines around the two hemispheres North and South of the equator, placed a dot on the map where she approximated the village from her dream to be. Then taking a ruler, Shala marked out where the other points might be, on a slightly compressed sphere like the Earth. As she touched the pencil to the map placing the final dot, her phone rang.

"Hi Angie, where have you been?" asked Shala, twirling the pencil through her fingers distractedly while looking intently at some of the areas she felt contained other vortexes.

"Hey Shala, Regression has been sick and I've been back and forth to the vet with him. What's up?" Angie had decided not to tell Shala, or anyone for that matter, about her awakening. Without a word of condolence for Regression, Shala launched into her monologue.

"So anyway, you know my re-occurring dream, right? Well, I've figured out the message. The native woman enters some kind of cosmic portal, I'm sure of it. There's at least eight of them on the planet."

"Wow! That's cool. Let's meet for coffee on Friday morning so you can give me the full run down," said Angie, quite interested.

"Looking forward to it. Love you."

Angie, placed the phone back in its cradle beside her bed and resting her left hand on her belly and right hand on her chest, closed her eyes and watched the gentle dance of prana as it scintillated through her body. *I feel like a little battery on recharge. I've been run down for years. I certainly need to help others recharge once I'm ready. This is exciting*!

After about twenty minutes, she rolled onto her side and drifting into slumber, dreamt of spiral galaxies floating in an infinite cosmic ocean; tiny cells in the vast universal body of consciousness.

The following week was rather uneventful for Angie. Her main focus was to balance her increased awareness and sensitivity to the environment with her growing understanding of the power awakening within her. Archer hadn't phoned and Angie got the feeling he probably wouldn't. Although he no doubt had the best sex of his life with her the previous weekend, Angie read it in his eyes as he was leaving that she was now too much for him to handle.

On Friday morning Angie was sitting waiting for Shala, a cup of rosehip tea in her hands, her eyes closed and her mind calm. She felt Shala enter the little café and opened her eyes to watch her place a huge book down onto the little coffee table. Opening it to the centre and placing her finger on a small pencil dot she exclaimed, "I need to find this village!"

"What's it called?' asked Angie, before taking another sip of her tea.

"I don't know," said Shala, as she placed her handmade Napalese handbag on the floor.

"Is that new?" asked Angie, referring to the bag.

"I just love everything Nepalese at the moment." Shala rolled back her sleeves to reveal some stone bracelets. "They're just like the ones from my dream. I'm getting some yak hide moccasins too, they're on order – custom made!"

Angie looked at the dot and read a name beside it. "Annapurna. That's a mountain, isn't it?" She moved her finger to the East along the mountain range – Mt. Everest. "How are you going to locate the village?"

"Serendipity!" Shala beamed at Angie, her eyes flashing. "The universe will guide me somehow, in someway. All I have to do is stay focused and the answer will be presented."

"I take it though that this is just an approximation. How many tiny villages do you think there could be around this area?" Angie had never felt so clear and calm in Shala's presence before.

"Hard to say, really. I will of course be doing a lot of research and contacting different people who have travelled around there," said Shala, slumping back in her chair, the enormity of what she was planning draining her energy.

"Sorry. I didn't mean to drag you down. It's quite exciting. Tell me more of your latest dreams. What's been happening?" Angie knew this would perk her up and, without missing a beat, Shala sat forward again and launched into a blow-by-blow account of the last week's dreamscapes and their hidden meanings and messages.

"So what does Trevor think of the idea of you going to Nepal to find this village?" asked Angie quite pointedly.

"He's passively supportive I guess you could say."

"Is he going with you?" asked Angie with one raised eyebrow, not quite picturing Trevor being all that interested.

"I doubt it. I haven't invited him. This is my trip," said Shala, with no room for misinterpretation. "This is my soul's journey. Me following my inner guidance for a higher purpose!" her chin held high.

"It all sounds very exciting," said Angie, seeing Shala for the precocious, but sweet child she was. "When will you start making travel plans?"

"Well, that's the problem. It could take weeks or even months before I know exactly where I am going. I will apply for a Nepalese Visa next week. Hey, if it works out in your holidays, would you be interested in joining me?"

Angie looked into Shala's eyes and knew that it had just occurred to her to ask. "If the timing works out, that would be really cool for sure!" Angie looked around the café, then lowered her voice and leant forward conspiratorially. "How much do you think it would cost and how long do we go for?"

"They're the two questions I've been asking myself also," responded Shala, all pretension having exited her disposition. "Once I've located the village and we know exactly where we'll be going, I'd like to spend at least a month there. So including getting there and back I would say at least six weeks total. Return airfare and expenses probably will cost about four thousand each to be comfortable. I mean we could do it cheaper, but not by much." Then it was Shala's turn to look around furtively. "I don't have any money saved right now, but I do have some savings bonds my parents got me for my education, when I was ten years old. I'm thinking of cashing them in. I believe it's about two and a half grand."

Angie thought of her travel plans. *Four grand in six weeks. Yikes! I wanted to be gone for half a year on that amount. Maybe unrealistic, but if I stayed on in India... hmmm.* "I guess we'll just see how everything pans out. I still have a month of school anyway," said Angie, as she finished the last of her tea.

"You seem really different!" said Shala, really looking at Angie's face for the first time. "Your skin is glowing. You look like you've lost weight too," she said checking Angie out a little bit more. "You look gorgeous!" she finished, and she meant it.

Angie blushed, but held Shala's gaze. "Thanks Shala. I feel good. I've been getting a lot of rest and I've cut out dairy products. I think the spring air is helping too!"

"Well, whatever it is, it's working for you. You want to go down to the river? A quiet stroll through the watershed. Lots of new blossoms have started to appear!"

"Sounds wonderful. Let's go."

Shala was quite surprised since Angie would normally have some excuse not to go. *Something is very different,* thought Shala, as she closed the huge atlas and picked up her bag.

The following day, Angie was sitting in meditation at the end of her Saturday morning yoga class and found herself reliving moments from the morning lecture with Dr. Opinski; recollections at the book-signing table when David had looked her in the eyes. This time, with strong determination, he said, "Call me!" It gave Angie quite a shock. Angie replayed the scene in her mind. *His eyes look different now. Has he fallen in love with me? That's ridiculous.* However, she couldn't shake the feeling that right now, two weeks after their initial encounter, David had decided Angie was the girl he had been waiting for. *This is interesting,* she thought. Angie let her own feelings flush through her body. *I am very attracted to him for sure. How old is he I wonder? He should be back in town this weekend. Maybe I'll give him a call.*

Angie let go of all mental chatter, allowing her mind to drift like a feather on the breeze, waves of loving energy washing over her as she finished her practice with *meta;* sending love and gratitude out into the world.

Angie rolled up her yoga mat and headed into the carpark. She unlocked her car, opened the passenger door, placed her bag and yoga gear on the passenger seat, then rummaged around in her bag for her phone. From the side-pocket, she removed her signed copy of David's book and opened it to the page where the slip of paper with his number acted as her bookmark. Angie stood there for what seemed an eternity, as she second-guessed her decision to call him.

Why am I making this into such a big deal? Because if he likes me as much as I now think he does and I like him as much as I think I might, then that could be very serious. I don't know anything about him. He doesn't know anything about me. He thinks I'm attractive and that I am planning to go traveling. I have been enjoying his book and it is definitely unlocking some very deep intelligence within me. Maybe he has experienced similar awakenings? That would be cool. More than just a theorist. I guess he has to keep his ideas fairly hypothetical or he would be shunned as a crackpot. The science seems fairly sound from what I have read so far. Blending Eastern mysticism with Western science is no new trick.

A quick call to let him know I am free today and tomorrow. It's ringing. Hopefully I get his message bank.

"Hello, David speaking."

"Hi David, it's Angie. You gave me your…"

"Hello. I am so happy you called. How are you?"

"I'm really good, thanks," replied Angie, relaxing considerably. "Are you in town?"

"Yes, I'm staying at…" Angie heard some paper rustling "The Hyatt Regency on 4th and 7th."

"I know the one."

"Would you like to meet for lunch? If you're not busy?" asked David.

"Lunch would be great. How about the lobby at 12pm," said Angie, realizing it was only 8am. "Hope I didn't call too early. I forgot how early the Mysore class is."

"Oh no, I have my own early morning exercise regimen also," said David, as he walked to the kitchenette and grabbed an iced tea out of the fridge.

"Yoga?" asked Angie.

"More like a blend of Chi Qong and Karate; very slow deliberate sequences. A moving meditation nonetheless." David was very excited to hear Angie's voice.

"Nice. Well, I guess we can chat more later," said Angie, the adrenaline still coursing through her veins.

"Perfect. See you then."

"Excellent. Bye." Angie threw her phone onto the seat and stood there next to her little car drinking in the warmth of the morning sun.

Life is so beautiful and precious, she thought, her heartbeat slowly returning to normal. *I can traverse the universe in my mind, sit in a state of perfect knowing, but still my heart races and my palms sweat when a new boy comes calling.*

Chapter Three - Rarefied Air

Anthony and Katelyn were having breakfast not far from camp, situated a few kilometers northwest of Tang Ting, the little Nepalese village which had seen a thousand-fold increase in Westerners over the last two years, ever since HPM Quarterly did a feature article on the bizarre energy anomaly on the mountain, now towering above them and glinting in the early morning sun.

Human Potential Movement (HPM) Quarterly had been sent a translation of a diary, purportedly found in a backpack left by an unknown traveler, in what had then been an abandoned hut on the Southern end of the main road through Tang Ting. Mountain climbers had a history of leaving gear they were never going to use again, many of them thinking of it as a donation to the local economy. The locals didn't have much use for the gear and it was extremely rare for any other mountaineers to need anything they hadn't packed in themselves. However, that was in the early days, before the HPM Quarterly article. Now you could arrive practically naked if you wanted, everything you needed could be found in one of the three outfitters now operating in the once unknown little village.

It was however a very remote village geographically. Taking over two and a half days by bus from Bahraich, just over the Indian border. There was of course the once a week helicopter drop, but unless you had a spare $6,000 each way, bus it was. This previously unspoiled pristine part of the world was now suffering the ravages of the tourism industry: waste management, profit's ugly twin. The spine-jarring bus ride from Bahraich only operated once the road was cleared of snow in late May, and ended its run usually sometime in September, before the new snow started to fall in earnest. In Spring the road was often cut by mudslides and avalanches, when late season snow was dumped on top of sheets of ice warmed by the sun then frozen again at night. The weather patterns in this part of the world were some of the most unpredictable and treacherous found anywhere on the planet.

Anthony turned to Katelyn, a huge grin on his face, as he munched his granola and maca powder breakfast bar. "I can't believe we're here in one piece. This is so awesome!" Katelyn loved Anthony's enthusiasm for life and had been with him on numerous adventures over the last four years. Katelyn had met Anthony not long before his born-again Christian experience, and, once they had a strong relationship foundation, had asked him 'please limit the Jesus talk, just a little bit'. Katelyn knew this was going to be a huge challenge for Anthony, but more important was her need to avoid the emotional reaction she had every time he would launch into a Jesus rant.

"I know. I'm so excited. I can't believe that up on that mountainside is an area of such powerful psychic energy. Two years and we're finally here!" Katelyn too was beaming; this trip after all was her idea.

"I hope you find what you're looking for Katelyn," said Anthony honestly.

"Thanks Anthony. Whatever happens up there, I'm open. The clarity of mind I'm feeling right now is exquisite. I wish I could feel like this everyday. Shame we have to travel thousands of miles from home to feel this good." She laughed, making light of the situation. Katelyn found it hard to feel the enormity of her emotions and often preferred to reign them in. "If the destination is anything like the journey itself, then I'm in for a wild ride!"

"Indeed," responded Anthony, as he gazed at the surrounding mountain range. "One more day of rest and then it's your turn."

Not wanting to think about tomorrow morning's rendezvous with the energy vortex, Katelyn changed the subject. "How about we hire a couple of bikes and take that circuit we were reading about yesterday?"

"Sounds good to me" said Anthony, as he jumped to his feet and put out his hand for Katelyn. Pulling her to her feet, he bent down and placed a few items, including their passports, in the daypack and handed it to Katelyn. "I'll run this other pack up to the locker, grab some more supplies and meet you at the bike rental shop."

"Thanks. See you in twenty." Katelyn secured the strap on the daypack across her chest and walked briskly towards the southern track that wound back into town, as Anthony headed off in the opposite direction. Theft was high, so there were several small huts with lockers for the storage of valuables. Passports of course were recommended to be kept on one's person at all times. Some of the thieving was initiated by a gang of local boys, but most of it was perpetrated by other travelers. Food was the most common item to disappear. Expensive, and untraceable once consumed, it was also a black market currency. Travelers were advised to bring as much food as possible for the duration of their stay. The helicopter supply drop, although scheduled to arrive once a week, was very weather dependent. The helicopter had been over three weeks late on several occasions and two climbers had died from injuries received in falls, waiting for rescue.

That evening, several pilgrims (as they were referred to by climbers) were sharing their day's experiences from time spent at the portal. Each of the three was from various countries in Europe and they were conversing in English; their common tongue. Katelyn was pretending not to listen as she waited for Anthony to return from the storage locker. She was half reading an article in a National Geographic she found laying next to the couch in the communal recreation hall, around which the camp was situated.

"It vas amazing. I *huff* never felt such a sense of my own creative potential. Images of sacred geometric shapes were unlocking regions of my brain, which normally lay dormant."

"Yes, I know exactly what you say. I saw these similar shapes also. One shape, a stellated icosohedron, was bouncing around just outside my body. I would say, in my *auric field*, and it was throwing up images of what I think was past lives."

"Yes, that is a very strong theme, so I've heard. Past lives, lives of the local villagers too, the chosen ones, who enter the portal. I felt such a strong desire to jump the barrier!" They all laughed heartily at this comment, for it is what everybody feels, but so few want to admit. The desire is wrapped in the fear of the legend of never being seen again.

"I wonder where they go?"

"Curiosity kills the cat, as they say."

"Have you heard the theory there are other portals?"

"Yes, people are trying to find these other places. Have any been found, do you know?"

"No. Maybe you can use these portals to move around from place to place on the planet. This is what some people think."

"A naturally occurring teleportation machine. Very cool!" Again, more laughter.

There's got to be more to it than this, thought Katelyn. Either people can't articulate their experiences very well, or it's just another new age joy ride. Katelyn had a healthy skepticism, but also longed for a deep spiritual connection to something larger than her own imaginings.

The threesome of pilgrims continued chatting, and Katelyn continued pretending not to listen. More images and feelings were shared. *Well, I've got my chance tomorrow. I hope it's beyond anything I've ever experienced before,* thought Katelyn.

Placing the National Geographic on the floor beside the couch, Katelyn stood up and made her way to the end of the hall, where the back door lead to the outside toilet. "Do you have a focus pendant?" asked a woman, sitting by herself on the floor at the end of the hall. It took Katelyn a second to register the words; the woman's accent was very thick.

"Sorry? Were you talking to me?"

"Yes. Do you have a focus pendant?"

"Ah, no, and without sounding rude, I guess you're going to try to sell me one?" Katelyn put her hand on the door and began to push it open into the cool night air.

"No. I do not sell them. I watch you listening to their stories." The woman pointed her gnarled walking stick to the three young men still chatting down the other end of the hall. "I hear the same stories repeated endlessly by every pilgrim who comes. They come for thrills mainly, you see. Go somewhere new. Get a buzz. This is not bungee jumping." The last two words came from the woman's mouth like liquid poison, and Katelyn felt suddenly queasy.

"Sorry Miss. I did not mean to scare you. You have a good heart and good intentions. I want you to have a purposeful experience. I wait here for someone like you. Those that seek something deeper. If you want to go deep, I recommend a focus pendant. If you want one, you come with me." Katelyn still felt uneasy. This woman, although partially hidden by shadow, had the presence of someone who knew many secrets. Ancient wisdom.

"I would have to tell my traveling companion..."

"Forget him. He has found his truth. He is here for you. Follow me now and we visit an old friend who will craft for you your pendant." The woman looked up at Katelyn from under the brim of a farmer's straw hat.

Transfixed by the woman's gaze, Katelyn felt she was frozen in eternity, held in this moment until she acquiesced to the woman's request. She heard her own voice ask robotically, "How long will it take?"

Hearing this, the woman sprang to her feet, and gently pushed on Katelyn's elbow, ushering her out into the darkness. "Not long. There is only one stipulation. You must not under any circumstances cross over the little safety barrier you will see when you get to the portal tomorrow. Come my friend, my home is this way."

Katelyn thought of Anthony and wanted desperately to go to their tent and let him know where she was going, or at least tell him she would be back later, but she knew this could not be.

I will just have to trust this crotchety old woman.

Anthony arrived at the hall only minutes after Katelyn had exited with the old crone. Not seeing Katelyn anywhere in the hall, he walked to a table and asked the two girls chatting there if they had seen her, and gave them a brief description. "Yes, I saw her walk towards that door", said one of the girls as she turned, half in her chair, and pointed to the door, leading to the toilets outside. "Probably about five minutes ago," she finished, pre-empting Anthony's next question.

"Thanks very much." He smiled at the two girls and they smiled back. He then turned and headed for the couch where Katelyn had been sitting and picked up the National Geographic, expecting her to be back any minute. Opening to the same article, he read, '*The Portal of Creation, as it is being called, came to the awareness of the new age movement after the translation from the firsthand account had been published in HPM Quarterly. It is claimed the story is of unknown penmanship as no one has yet come forward admitting to having written it. The diary had been found in a pack in an abandoned shack by two Austrian mountaineers over two years ago.*

The Austrian couple had kept the diary more as a curiosity than anything of importance, as neither of them were able to decipher the Italian handwriting. It wasn't until several months later, and purely by chance, that a fellow mountaineer from Italy read the title on the cover of the diary, whilst sharing a room with the Austrians in the Swiss Alps.

After ascertaining the diary was not one of theirs, the Italian asked if she could read it, since she had nothing in her native tongue left to read. After almost a year from the date of the last entry, a story began to unfold.'

Anthony looked up from the magazine and turned to the back of the hall. *Maybe she went back to our tent from the outhouse. She'll probably come back here when she sees I'm not there*, he thought, turning back to the article.

'Olivia Staglioni spent several months transcribing into English what she had read in the small leather bound diary. She then shopped the manuscript around to a number of publishing houses in the hopes of a publishing deal for the story she claimed was a work of fiction. After a year of rejections, she then sent the manuscript to HPM Quarterly having updated the preface with a true account of the story's existence.

Olivia had never validated the whereabouts of the energy vortex, but had a vague recollection of the approximate location from the Austrian couple's description. It wasn't until Otto Schwartz, the original mountaineer to discover the diary, happened to hear a news-clip on the story, that the location of the village was revealed. It was then easy to locate the portal from the description in the diary.'

The main door opened and Anthony looked up hoping to see Katelyn smiling back at him. Instead, standing in the doorway was Davo, the Australian owner of the whitewater rafting company which operated tours in the class four rapids further upstream. After spotting the two girls Anthony had spoken to earlier, Davo waved to them. As the two girls passed Anthony, one put her hand on his shoulder saying, "she has not returned," as a statement but actually asking a rhetorical question like many Europeans who speak English as their second or third language.

"Probably went looking for me I guess, and we passed each other in the dark," said Anthony warmly. "She'll no doubt come back here." The girls headed towards the door as Davo tipped his imaginary hat in Anthony's direction. Anthony give him the peace sign, fingers raised in a V, as the three of them left.

Anthony took another look around the hall. Four separate groups of climbers were standing around or leaning on various pieces of furniture throughout the hall. The three guys Katelyn had been eavesdropping on earlier and another group of pilgrims were chatting amiably on two couches facing each other in the back left corner. Climbers were easy to distinguish from pilgrims, as they always wore their expensive Gortex jackets. Most of the climbers went to the vortex of energy to see what all the fuss was about, but none of the pilgrims did any mountaineering. Pilgrims were here for only one reason only - potential enlightenment. There had been a whole new section in the back of HPM Quarterly, dedicated to pilgrim experiences at the portal. As with many new age experiences, outrageous claims could be read in the numerous published accounts over the past year.

Anthony looked at his watch: 8:23pm. *It's still too early for bed, surely she would have made the round trip to the tent and back by now. Hmmm, I'll just stay here, otherwise we'd probably end up playing cat and mouse all night.*

Anthony turned his attention back to the National Geographic article describing the history of the little village which had so suddenly been transformed by the tourist industry. '*Tang Ting has maintained its cultural heritage for more than eight hundred years, practicing the shamanic tradition of the Bon which has fallen victim to Buddhism in so many other villages throughout this part of the world. Little is understood of the rituals this particular village practice in relation to the energy vortex and fact is hard to separate from fiction in the fantastical realm of metaphysical experience.*

Numerous reporters have interviewed nearly all of the hundred or so villagers over the past year. Still the mystery remains as to the true spiritual practices of this anachronistic village. Although mountaineers have been passing through here since the nineteen thirties to climb Annapurna to the Northeast, it has never been anything more than a place to rest, prepare and acclimatize to the rarefied air of this altitude. In Tang Ting, food is scarce and as many of the locals who can leave, do.

Anthony put down the magazine and walked over to the hand pump at the sink and filled his canteen with the glacier melt water from the roof's holding tank. The water tasted sweet as it quenched his considerable thirst. He reflected on the day's bike ride, and decided the few breaks they had to rehydrate were obviously not adequate. *It really is so dry up here,* he thought, as he took another long draught on the heavenly beverage. Filling the canteen once more, he screwed on the plastic cap and returned to his seat. Flicking through the remaining pages of the article, he saw some beautiful photos of the wild landscape and scanned a couple of the mini sub-headings for anything else of interest. The last three paragraphs were preceded by the title *Potential Transformation*, and so Anthony read on, curious as to the nature of the information.

Katelyn had been lead along a familiar path to the North, which then forked after several minutes of brisk walking, to the East, toward the only place any of the tourists were not permitted to enter.

"I'm not allowed down here," she said, as they wound their way down to the river.

"It's okay missy. You're invited this time," said the old woman, again looking up from underneath the brim of her hat, the light of the half-moon glinting in her eyes. "You're on special business and under my wing. No one will challenge you here as long as you are with me. We have been waiting for you." These last words hung in the still air below the level of the plane, like a menacing fog.

Katelyn stopped and tried to extricate herself from the diminutive woman's grip on her elbow. No luck. The grip was not painful, just simply immovable.

"There is nothing to fear, but we need to move fast. Forces are aligning against us and you my dear have a role to play. Come, there is much to do before your time at the portal tomorrow." Without further protestation Katelyn was again walking into the one area she had been told not to go.

A few days prior the orientation guide had pointed to the map and explained, *"This area here is the camp of the shamans. None of them are at all happy about the discovery of their sacred object, and out of respect for their privacy, all foreigners are forbidden to enter their camp. It's marked on all the local maps and there is signage on all the paths leading to their homes."* Katelyn remembered turning to Anthony after this, only moments after their arrival, pulling an exaggerated grimace of apprehension, which said *'Geez, that's heavy,'* neck muscles strained, the edges of her mouth pulled downwards, teeth bared.

Katelyn stumbled on a river rock she did not see in the pale moonlight. "So sorry," said the woman without slowing her pace. Katelyn had then been thinking of Anthony and sending him loving vibes. *"My adventure's happening Anthony. Please don't worry. Give me until morning. I'll be alright. Whatever you do, don't come looking for me."*

Katelyn was in her mid thirties, capable and enduring. At home she was a yoga instructor and had been to India numerous times over the past ten years, leading and participating in yoga workshops. The last time was as a teacher assisting in a yoga training course in Rishikesh. That was when she first heard of the Portal of Creation.

With olive skin, brown hair down to her waist, and dark brown eyes, Katelyn blended easily in the hubbub of Asia. She was well travelled and had forsaken marriage – several requests – as well as a mortgage, for her passion to travel. However, she didn't see herself as a tourist, but as a free spirit with the God-given right to experience the wonders of her beautiful world.

Katelyn's God was not the old man God of her childhood. Katelyn's God was the indescribable power of the universe. The mystical, magical energy of creation. Katelyn's experiences of the power and truth of this energy had moved her to tears on numerous occasions during yoga, meditation, hiking, making love, and during her favourite past time of ecstatic shaking. Katelyn's God was the truth of the felt presence of immediate reality and she loved everything that could put her in greater contact with the immutable now.

The old woman lead Katelyn over a short bridge, only a few meters above the roaring water below, and up a steep incline to an area encircled by numerous small huts. In the centre of the clearing was a modest fire and around the fire Katelyn saw eight pairs of eyes staring up at her, the whites of these eyes glowing brightly in the firelight.

The diminutive woman exchanged several rapid bursts of staccato sounds with two of the tribes people squatting there, who then sprang to their feet and hurried toward one of the huts. Katelyn looked up at the moon and then at the silhouette of the snowcapped peaks, a smattering of stars twinkling wanly between small low clouds. Taking a couple of deep breaths, she thought to herself, *this is magical.* She closed her eyes, drinking in the sounds and smells of her surroundings. "Perfect. Beyond plans lies the serendipity of life," she whispered, quoting a favourite mantra. She opened her eyes as she heard the soft padding of approaching feet.

Another brief exchange between Gwylin and one of the tribes people and she was again moving, this time towards the hut into which she had seen the two figures disappear. At five-foot nine inches tall, Katelyn had to stoop to make it through the hut's low yak skinned opening. Straightening up slowly in the hopes of not hitting her head, Katelyn peered around the hut in the dim light cast from the small flickering fire in the centre of the dirt floor, her eyes beginning to water from the smoky dry, warm air. Katelyn was pulled down onto some soft animal hides, by the little woman who then drew a hand gently down over her eyes in a signal for her to close them. Katelyn obliged.

Low rhythmic chanting began and continued for several minutes. Katelyn could hear the soft rustle of the hides as several more people entered the hut and sat on the floor. More voices were added to the chanting. Then came the clear ring of a brass bell and the chanting stopped. Katelyn pictured the small Tibetan bells joined by their leather strap which she had on an altar in her yoga studio back home. A small squeeze on her thigh from the woman who had guided her here and she opened her eyes. *The smoke is certainly less bothersome down on the floor,* she thought. Out of the shadows on the other side of the fire-pit came a deep growl and the head of a wolf, teeth bared in an expression of menace as adrenaline hit her like a punch to the chest. Knowing she had no chance of escape, she raised her hands like claws and bared her own teeth in the same fashion and growled back. She heard a cheer and the animal faded back into the darkness of the hut. Before Katelyn had time to register what had taken place, a face appeared. A serene face, *the face of a Buddha,* she thought. In a deep musical voice it said, "Welcome!"

Anthony finished the article, checked his watch once again, looked around the hall one last time, got off the couch, headed out the front door and back towards their campsite. "She's a big girl," he said to the cool night air. "She can look after herself," he whispered to the stars twinkling overhead as he made his way to their tent.

He knelt down and took hold of the zipper to open his tent, when a voice in the shadows said, "She will stay with the shamans this night. She is safe."

"Thank you," responded Anthony after regaining his composure. The voice had given him quite a fright, as he had been completely unaware of the presence of another human being. Anthony took off his boots, entered his tent, closed the flap on the fly, took off his jacket and pants and climbed into his sleeping bag. Lying on his back with his eyes closed he pictured Jesus floating above his tent in a radiance of pure white light and asked that he protect Katelyn and help guide her on her journey. "Amen," he said quietly in the stillness of the night, before rolling over and drifting off to sleep.

Katelyn sat in the dim light cast from the small fire, and listened to the woman who had brought her, speak in her native tongue to the other people sitting quietly in the circle. It was obvious to Katelyn the woman was talking about her, but of course what was being said was a complete mystery. The few phrases of the local dialect she had taught herself were only good for morning and evening greetings, name exchange and asking simple directions; none of which were of any use at that moment.

There was however one word which had been spoken numerous times, which Katelyn imagined to be a name for the energy vortex. "*Quantao,*" she repeated in her mind the next time it was spoken. She thought of Quan Yin, the Goddess of compassion, as her mnemonic device.

The woman turned to Katelyn. "My name's Gwylin. This means Mountain Tamer." From across the hut came the basso rumble of distant rolling thunder. It took Katelyn a moment to realize the sound was English. More words were uttered, "My name is Bon Chen Tsang Pao. I am your guide this night. Please accept this gift, it will aid you greatly this coming day." Katelyn noticed movement amongst the shadowy figures as something was passed anti-clockwise around the circle. She put out her two hands as a stone the size of a peach was placed into them. Her hands were closed around the object and then guided towards her chest by the person beside her. Katelyn made eye contact and smiled as she nodded her head in acceptance, the giver simply turned and bowed his head, assuming his previous posture.

Katelyn was subtly feeling the object with her thumbs and could sense markings on one side. Gwylin spoke again, "This is ancient power object, born before mountains. Please look now." Katelyn brought her hands to eye level, turning them to catch the firelight. The object was dark but highly polished. Tracing her index finger over the markings and catching the pale light just right, she could make out a faint spiral as it wound its way over the slightly convex surface. Just as Katelyn had worked out what it must be, Bon Chen grumbled, "Fossilized sea snail." Katelyn nodded. "This is focus pendant. It has been tuned to your vibration. It will guide your spirit." He uttered something else, which Katelyn did not understand, but movement in the shadows signaled its intent. A leather thong had been produced and threaded through a small hole in the fossil. The leather was then tied behind her neck and the fossil placed on her chest. As she glanced down, Katelyn could clearly see the spiral on this ancient creature's home, as it wound its way to the raised centre.

Chanting once again filled the hut, but this time it was accompanied by an intricate rhythm played on a single drum. Katelyn closed her eyes and felt the weight of the fossil on her breastbone. The rhythm of the drum seemed to be talking to something very old within her chest, the fossil acting like a small amplifier, boosted the signal as it resonated with her ribcage. Katelyn began seeing geometric patterns shimmering behind her closed eyelids. *Ancient wisdom. Secrets revealed,* came the words unbidden to her mind *relax and flow.*

Katelyn eventually became aware of the silence and opened her eyes. She looked around her to find an empty hut and a small pile of glowing embers in the firepit. Moments later Gwylin entered through the hides and knelt beside her. Gwylin uttered some words, which Katelyn figured to be a prayer or incantation, and then threw something onto the fire. A pungent mix of smells filled the small hut and left Katelyn's olfactory working overtime as she tried to decode some of the scents. All Katelyn could be sure about was the smell of sage, which she had seen growing along the trails on the previous days bike ride. Beginning to feel the aches in her knees, ankles and thighs she wondered what the time might be. As if reading her mind, Gwylin said, "It is time to go." Gwylin helped Katelyn to her feet and pressed expertly in several pressure points around Katelyn's knees and then two more in the small of her back, as she bent low to get outside.

Expecting darkness, Katelyn was quite disoriented to step into the brightness of the new day sun directly in front of her, low in the valley sky and amplified as it reflected off the river winding around the little camp.

Closing her eyes, Katelyn breathed in the serenity of the moment as she focused herself on the enormity of her hopes for deep connection on this special day. "What providence to be singled out by the local shamans," she whispered. Sensing Gwylin's presence waiting patiently beside her, she asked quietly, "Why was I chosen?"

"I have dreamed you for several moons, you are one of sixteen needed to fulfill the final prophecy. Time is running out but today is your day. You have been cleansed and purified to the best of our abilities. I will take you to the path beyond our home that will lead you to the mountain." With that said, Gwylin reached out and took Katelyn's hand and they both walked through the clearing towards the path which lead over the narrow bridge spanning the churning river.

Due to the overwhelming influx of visitors who come to view the energy anomaly, a pre-register and session time allocation system has been established to assert a semblance of order to the proceedings. Registration of one's desire to visit the portal is logged during an application for visa entry into Nepal. Session times are generated during the orientation meeting upon arrival in Tang Ting. During the peak season months of July and August, each visitor has a half hour personal encounter with the energy vortex. There is a safety fence with warning signs in numerous languages, describing the penalty of maximum jail time and monetary fines for proceeding beyond the perimeter. On the safe side is an area about twelve feet long and four feet wide, which narrows to the opening that leads out onto the side of the mountain. From here the path snakes its way precariously down to the valley below. Inside, the chamber is lit by an array of LED's powered by a small solar panel mounted outside, above the opening.

Katelyn stood just inside the cave entrance, sensing the power of the vortex and gauging her emotional and physiological responses to its presence. She had heard of the vision distortions experienced by many others when standing at the safety railing, but at her current distance she was experiencing only goose-bumps and a mixture of excitement and mild apprehension.

Katelyn had a plan for her approach, and after the encounter with the shamans gifting her the focus pendant, she decided to be extremely diligent in its execution. Her plan was simple: move one small step at a time and observe any and all changes as they occur. She wanted to allow ten minutes to cover the short distance to the railing, fifteen minutes at the fence and five minutes retreat, to prevent any possible ill-effects due to exiting the energy field too quickly.

Several minutes in, each step taken closer to the vortex increased exponentially the effects she was experiencing. The visual distortions had started much sooner than expected. The electrical energy from the Chi moving through her meridians had made her dizzy, forcing her to stop twice and regain her composure and she was not even one-third of the way there.

"Maybe this focus pendant is too strong for me," she said aloud. "This is too intense. Just breathe." Katelyn bounced up and down on the balls of her feet and shook her arms to help get the Chi flowing. "I've come a long way and trained as best I can." She thought of all the intent she had put into her yoga over the last six months. "Breathe and move forward" she whispered to the musty air. Her words were swallowed by the cold stone of the cave.

At the halfway point, she reached up with her left hand and touched the fossilized sea snail. *It is definitely warmer than the ambient temperature,* she noted, and looking down at the spiral saw it glowing with a neon blue light, pulsing in a slow rhythmic pattern. She brought her right hand up to her neck and felt her pulse. She knew how to proceed; *I need to synchronize my heartbeat to the fossil's pulse.*

Katelyn spent the next five minutes inching her way forward as she slowed her heart rate to match that of the pulsing blue spiral. She was now two-thirds of the way to the safety fence as she lifted her gaze from the pendant. The portal was iridescent and shimmering. A kaleidoscope of symmetry and energy in an intricate dance of enfolded colours. It was as though someone had taken a rainbow arch and crumpled it like a piece of paper. The topology looked infinite in complexity but seemed to follow specific rules of interplay and geometry. Katelyn thought of the numerous fractal art generators she had played with, *but this occupies three dimensional space. I wonder if anyone has been able to smuggle a camera past the security guard? This would make the best picture. Put this on the front of a magazine!*

Closing her eyes to check in with herself again, she decided all systems were operating without resistance. Her emotions were clear and joyous, her physiological processes seemed normal now; no sweat or overheating. She felt chi pumping around her body and could taste a build up of sweet nectar on the back of her tongue. *Ambrosia of the Gods,* she mused. *Divine!*

Katelyn opened her eyes and checked her pulse against that of the flashing blue spiral, and made the minute adjustment to bring them back into phase. She could feel tingles running around her scalp as her ears popped in equalization and could then discern a faint hissing emanating from the portal. She moved closer, her steps bigger as the joy increased. The tingling in her scalp moved down her arms and torso and started spreading over her legs. Her cells began to coruscate as waves of electricity enveloped her.

The observer part of Katelyn noticed a greater level of spatial connectedness. Time had essentially come to a standstill as her body merged with the power and enormity of the mountain. As she took the final step to the safety fence she recalled the warning Gwylin had whispered to her earlier that morning, *You must not enter the portal!* Every cell in her body was buzzing with the desire to leap into the vortex. *If I feel this good standing here...* Katelyn was caught off guard as a face emerged from the spiraling kaleidoscope of colours. She thought for a moment she was looking into a reflection of herself. She called out, "Who are you?" and a voice responded inside her head, *"Please take my hand. I can't make the final step."* Leaning as far forward over the railing as she possibly could, she reached for the outstretched hand. "Just a tiny bit more. Stretch!" yelled Katelyn, feeling like a heroine from a B-grade 1960's sci-fi movie.

Chapter Four - Between Worlds

Angie met David in the foyer of his hotel a little after 12pm. He was sitting by the fireplace, reading a magazine. She couldn't quite see which periodical it was and presumed incorrectly that it was a scientific journal. David looked up as she approached, the click-clack of her black leather ankle boots on the marble floor taking all the ninja stealth out of her light and languid step.

"Hello," said David as he placed the magazine on the coffee table and stood up. "You look stunning. No sweat pants today?" a cheeky grin upon his handsome face. Angie had deliberated for about half an hour what was appropriate attire for this meeting. They hadn't discussed where they were going to eat, but Angie figured a nice restaurant might be the choice. It was warm and sunny today, but depending on the restaurant it could be quite cold, as many establishments had turned their thermostats down by now. She decided on black tights under a short midnight-blue marino wool dress. Her hair out and freshly washed, lay luxuriously over a dark grey pashmina scarf. She clutched a small black hemp handbag with an embroidered butterfly in her left hand and wore silver butterfly earrings. Her arms were bare and she had decided that if it was going to be too cold and her scarf wasn't warm enough as a shawl, she would borrow David's jacket, rather than carrying one of hers around. Mascara, a light dusting of concealer on the cheeks and around the eyes to cover any small blemishes and a very light pink lip gloss, more for shine than anything else, was all the make-up she would allow.

Angie took his proffered hand in hers and held his gaze. Her heart was beating slightly faster than normal for the little amount of walking she had just done, and she could sense the deepened connection which had grown since their first encounter only a couple of weeks ago. *Interesting how time has this effect even on a relationship so new,* she thought and smiled.

"You don't look too bad yourself," she said, and glanced down at the table as David let go her hand and gestured towards the other over-stuffed lounge chair. *Interesting,* Rolling Stone Magazine, *never would have guessed that. Hopefully he has good taste in music too.*

"You seem really different Angie, beyond the make-up and clothes. You seem somehow younger but more worldly at the same time. How have you been?" *Something is very different,* he thought.

Angie didn't know where to start and the directness of his gaze made her feel both welcomed and apprehensive at the same time. *I don't want to scare him off with my experiences but he is asking and can sense something has changed. Do I tell him his book 'changed my life'? Ha! He is smart and I think he may know more about what I am experiencing than he has mentioned in his book. Keeping the mystical portion of his wisdom hidden behind science.*

"Well, to be honest, it has been quite the fortnight since we met, but before I launch into some of my crazy happenings, I would like you to give me an off the record version of your book. Something happened to you that your fellow scientists aren't seeing with their microscopes. Am I right?" David went a little pale and Angie liked it. *I knew it!* "Maybe we should go to your room? Oh, are you hungry? Sorry, I don't mean to be pushy but I would like to talk and here in the foyer, or even at a restaurant doesn't seem quite the right place."

"Do you like sushi?" asked David, "I can have them bring a platter to my room. What would you like to drink?"

"I love sushi, mainly tuna and salmon sashimi and anything with avocado in it. Mineral water would be great. Thank you," replied Angie, neither of them having broken eye contact since they sat down.

"Done. I will be back in a couple of minutes." David stood, smiled brightly and walked towards the restaurant at the far end of the foyer. Angie picked up the Rolling Stone magazine and flicked through the pages. There was an article on Keith Richards' book 'Occupy Earth' accompanied by a short interview. Angie thought of her dad, telling her she was named after the Rolling Stones song, and remembered how he had cried a little when he told her. She hadn't heard the song before and so he played it for her. '*It's so sad*' she had said as his tears fell. '*Yes, it's beautiful, like you pumpkin. Life is a bitter sweet mix of love and sadness.*' Angie was seven at the time, but she never forgot it. Her dad had never cried in her presence again.

Angie stood as David returned and handed him the magazine. "It was there when I came down," he said, placing it back on the table. "I was interested in reading the Keith Richards interview. He makes some insightful observations for a musician. It has been very interesting watching the occupy movement grow over the last six months. With millions of people now demonstrating all over the planet, I really wonder what the next steps will be. Europe is bankrupt and disintegrating, North America is on the brink of war with China over their debt obligations. The Federal Reserve, a privately owned bank, continually prints money without Congress' approval, placing their citizens into intractable debt. Maybe now with serious talk of the New Breton Woods Accord they can dig themselves out of the catastrophic financial mess they have created. It's hard to accept that the government really doesn't represent the people at all anymore. When corporations run the planet and military spending constitutes almost half of government expenditure, the people have no choice but to rebel."

"I basically live in a bubble these days when it comes to politics, and just hope our elected officials do the right thing. I place my vote but recognize the system is completely floored. I've personally had enough of all the lies and corruption. It's so obvious to me that an economic model based on debt obligations is unsustainable. When banks post billions of dollars in profits and then justify massive employee lay-offs in order to make more profits for the upcoming year you know a collapse is immanent." Angie smiled wanly and slipped her arm through his as if they had been friends forever. "Man I'm hungry!" she exclaimed, shifting the mood as they walked towards the elevator.

"You're right. Let's not talk of politics," said David as he pushed the button for the elevator. "Usually I would take the stairs but I am on the twenty-third floor. Thanks for coming, I was really hoping to see you again." A bell sounded, the doors opened and he followed Angie into the lift and pressed both the number 23 and the door close button. He stood back, taking her arm and placing it back where it had been. It felt so natural to both of them to be arm in arm with each other.

"I am about halfway through your book and I must admit much of it is going over my head. I haven't read a lot in the way of scientific literature recently, although I am familiar with some of the more popular ideas you discuss." She looked him in the eyes using the reflection of the elevator doors. "I think the TV sitcom, The Big Bang Theory helped, she said and smiled.

"I haven't heard of that one. I'll check it out sometime. I haven't had much time to watch TV in the last ten years or so."

"No doubt," replied Angie. "You're not missing much, but every now and again something good comes along. The nice thing these days is you can stream old episodes straight from the Internet. Very handy."

The bell sounded again, the doors opened and David steered them left and down the hall to his room. *He even smells good,* thought Angie, as David fished a key out of his jacket pocket. *Such a gentle and knowing presence about him too. Can't wait to hear his story.*

Entering the suite David took off his jacket and hung it in the closet by the door, removed his shoes and placed his room key on the coffee table between the two overstuffed blue chairs next to the huge bay window and gestured for Angie to sit. She took off her boots and sat, running her hands over the luxuriously soft fabric, as he walked to the kitchenette. David opened the fridge and was happily surprised to see room service had restocked it with juice, water, milk and some cans of pop. "Would you like something to drink while we wait for sushi?"

"Yes please. Water would be great, thanks." Angie looked out the window and down towards the river below. She noticed the ice along the river bank was nearly all gone and turned back to David as he brought two glasses of water to the table. He handed one to Angie. "Cheers," he said and Angie replied in kind.

"So you want to hear my story first. Fair enough, and you want the off the record version too. Promise you won't think I'm a mad scientist by the time we've finished. This is information I have shared with very few people. It would probably end my career if it got out that I thought this way about the world. No room for personal views or experience remember."

"I don't know about that. I think one's experience of the world is a clearer model to go by than what mathematical formulas and computer modeling might suggest. I know this is very unscientific, but I believe our bodily sense organs are the best instruments for measuring the world around us. I realize that of course that this is subjective knowledge and I remember you mentioned something about that in your lecture. I also don't believe in the Buddhist idea that this is all illusion either. I think our perception of reality can change and we should therefore be open to experiencing it in many different ways." As Angie finished saying this, there was a knock at the door.

"Perfect," said David as he walked to the door, opened it, accepted the platter of sushi and a small bottle of warmed saki, closed the door and returned, placing them on the table. He then went to the kitchenette and brought back two medium sized, matte-black square plates.

The presentation of the sushi was first class and the numerous cuts of tuna and salmon were large and ruddy. Angie's mouth was watering just looking at them. She scooped up a tablespoon amount of wasabi with the end of her chopsticks and then dolloped it onto her plate and not into the soy sauce, which was served in two small beige ceramic bowls. Angie preferred her wasabi straight and not mixed with soy sauce.

"Please help yourself," encouraged David as Angie paused for him to get settled.

"I'll sit on the floor if you don't mind. I think it will be easier," she said as she slid to the floor and pushed the table a little forward to give her more room. Smiling she continued, "This is better. It didn't feel right sitting as though I was from the Victorian age about to have a cup of tea. Now this feels more Japanese."

David joined her on the floor and moved several pieces of sashimi onto his plate and a few pieces of the different rolls he had ordered. "Dragon, California, Soft Shell Crab," he said pointing to each roll in turn, "and this one is a combination of Toro, spicy mayonnaise and avocado especially for you. Not sure if you like the belly of tuna but I hope so. Very delicious! Some people find it too oily, but not me."

"Yes, I like Toro," said Angie taking one to start. She placed it on her plate and smeared a little wasabi on it and then placed a tiny piece of pickled ginger over the wasabi. Without further ado she picked it up expertly with her chopsticks, dipped it in the soy sauce then placed it into her mouth, closed her eyes and bit down, letting the different flavours explode across her tongue, savouring every one of them.

David ate his first few pieces in silence and then said, "I guess I'll start at the very beginning. I was raised in a loving christian family but left the church around the age of sixteen. My intuition told me that Jesus' message was being twisted to fulfill human agendas, and the rhetoric I heard erased the deeper spiritual connection I yearned. I could only relate to Jesus as a man who had touched the Divine. The son of God in the same way we are all sons and daughters of God." David picked up a fat slice of tuna, dipped it into his soy sauce and then took a large bite.

Finishing the tuna sashimi he continued, "My interest in ancient Tibetan mysteries were piqued as a teenager, after reading the stories of T. Lobsang Rampa. A small group of us used to gather each Wednesday evening at the local library to discuss Indian and Tibetan teachings. I listened, studied and started meditating. The Tibetan system focused on the *nadis, Sushumna, Ida* and *Pingala,* how to charge the flow of *prana* in the *nadis,* the seven major *Chakras; Muladhara, Svadhishthana, Manipura, Anahata, Vishuddha, Ajna, Sahasrara,* and the mysterious serpent energy, *Kundalini.* It spoke of spiritual abodes like *Shambala* and other planes of existence." Taking a piece of salmon this time, his actions were repeated.

"I devoured all the material I could possibly find relating to spiritual unfolding. Of course this was all done in private as I was also studying for my undergraduate degrees in mathematics and physics. I continued with my spiritual quest and found a community of seekers through one of my professors. I was fortunate in meeting some local elders who possessed incredible knowledge handed down from generation to generation through the oral tradition of song. These songs were a powerful tool, and developed my understanding and experience of the nature and role of vibration in spiritual transformation. Strangely the experiences I was having in my meditations were similar to the quantum states I was studying and so I considered nothing too left field. Being with others who were older, more experienced and also meditating and discussing these ideas, I knew I was neither alone nor completely crazy for walking this path.

I continued to plough through the ancient texts and kept abreast of contemporary ground breaking theories and data. I started doing Tai Chi regularly and I also started doing Kundalini Yoga, which I found exhilarating. I refined my diet, removed dairy products and became a vegetarian. I moved into a large warehouse with about twelve other people after finishing my under graduate degrees and began working on my Master's thesis. These individuals were all focused on their own spiritual path and actively engaged in rigorous bodywork techniques. One of their favoured disciplines was Transformational Breathing, a technique developed by Dr. Stanislav Grof, the founder of the field of transpersonal psychology and a pioneering researcher into the use of altered states of consciousness for purposes of healing and insight".

"Yes, I am familiar with his work", said Angie her mouth half full of tuna.

"It was during a breath-work session that I became aware of a powerful dormant energy and its affects on my mind and body. I felt the energy moving through my meridians, and I also noticed where it was blocked and intuited what that meant on the physical, emotional, mental and spiritual levels of my being. I felt a profound tingling sensation in my lower back and had powerful spasms as electrical energy shot up my spine. I knew this to be the kundalini energy I had been studying and visualizing all these years. My first taste of the powerful transformations which take place when this energy is activated."

David glanced up at Angie at this moment and saw in her eyes that this too is what had happened to her since they first met.

"Please continue," she said, dipping another large slice of tuna into the soy sauce.

"Around this time I also met an interesting individual. I will not mention her name for sake of privacy but she acted as my guide and mentor. Symbolically, she showed me the key to unlocking the gate to the hidden mysteries of the Universe. She lived in a perfect small scale Great Pyramid laid out in its true orientation. Meditations and discourse in this magnificent yet humble abode helped open my third eye and I grokked the metaphysical path I was to tread in the not too distant future.

After completing my Masters' thesis I moved to Switzerland to test some theories at CERN and to work on my Ph.D. I also continued my physical cleansing and took it to new levels with an eight month course of colonic irrigations. Purging myself of all the toxic build-up of a meat eating diet put me on cloud nine. My skin shone with an inner glow similar to when I was a child; health radiating from every pore. My eyes got back their old sparkle and my mind lost its overlay of fogginess. Clarity is something you don't tend to notice losing but once it is restored the affects are fantastic. Every cell in my body seemed to vibrate with life force".

David ate some of the soft shell crab roll and nodded to Angie to try it next. "Delicious," he mumbled his mouth full. "Sorry. I am very impressed with the light tempura batter." Angie giggled and they ate in silence for a few minutes before he continued.

"All this cleansing was leading to the transcendental experience of my life, now only weeks away. I understood the neuro-chemical nature of mental health and I'd purified my blood through a healthy diet, avoiding intoxicants of any kind; refined sugars, saturated fats, animal protein were all long gone. I would never have guessed just how much my cellular wellbeing affected my consciousness. I had a good grasp of my neuromuscular attitude of armouring and how this sociopolitical role manifested my emotional state. I was finally leveling out the ups and downs of my emotional response to the social landscape and my place in it, consciously controlling the amplitude of how I felt. I was happy and full of life and energy. I was twenty-four years old, physically, emotionally and mentally as focused as I'd never been before.

Then one perfect still morning, doing freestyle Tai Chi at the edge of the lake down the road from my flat, I unexpectedly activated my latent kundalini energy, generating the opening of my chakras as it climbed my spine making its way to the crown of my head. It continued on climbing through half a dozen more chakras I didn't even know existed, until its journey was complete. I sat as a Buddha, for over four hours. Fortunately I wasn't working that day!", he laughed as he imitated Buddha's meditative style; eyes closed, big closed mouth grin on his face, hands resting on his knees, palms facing up with the thumb and forefinger forming a circle.

After opening his eyes he looked to Angie's empty plate. "You've slowed down, have you had enough, or are you just taking a break?" asked David, as Angie sat serenely, listening to him talk.

"Probably just taking a break, knowing my appetite," Angie laughed. "That's the curious thing about sushi, you get full so fast and are hungry again within the hour. Please continue. It is music to my soul to hear someone speak like this. Please give me the details."

"I was doing Tai Chi, beside the little lake near my home nestled in the mountains, as I had been most days since moving there about two months previous. The morning temperature was mild and the sky was a never-ending blue; not a cloud to be seen. The water was calm and the air was clean and crisp. I absolutely love those kind of days. My thoughts were focused on the beauty of my world, the indescribable joy of being alive and how fortunate I was to be here, able to enjoy the moment. As I settled into my routine and began circulating the chi around my body, bringing it up from the earth through the centers of my feet, I felt a tingling sensation at the base of my spine. I focused on this feeling as I continued to circulate the chi through my meridians.

As I mentioned earlier, I had felt similar sensations during my breath-work experiences. This electrical energy is unlikely to go unnoticed! As I was circulating the chi, which previously was more akin to visualizing the energy flowing than perhaps moving it around, I started to feel blockages dissolving. As the energy started flowing, and I certainly became aware of it flowing, I relaxed and went with the sensations as they occurred and spontaneously started humming. As I let the sound escape from my throat it began taking on a life of its own.

The sound was setting up resonant standing-waves within and around my body. The excitation of my being was now happening on many levels concurrently. Things started to unfold quickly and my thoughts flowed with a life of their own. I was finding the sensations a little overwhelming as the increased energy flowing within my body was generating a lot of heat, so I decided to walk down to the waters' edge and cool off.

I sat down and let the cool water lap over my feet. Sitting there, looking out at the horizon and feeling the energy continue to increase in intensity, my breathing started to synchronize with the rhythm of the waves as they lapped at the shore. I was also starting to see miniature points of white light dancing in front of my eyes. Their individual dance was brief but beautifully choreographed. They buzzed and pulsed and everywhere I turned my gaze I could see them. The air was becoming filled with them. Negative ions, prana, whatever we call them, I was becoming aware that they danced through my body as well.

My etheric or bio-electric body was really starting to tingle and as I moved my hands over my limbs and torso I could sense this new level of electrical charge. My thoughts were flowing with a speed and coherence that I had never experienced before. Not only was I processing the sensation of kundalini, noting the rise of this intense energy as it grew up my spine stimulating my chakras and opening doorways to long forgotten realms, but I was also aware of my thoughts, flowing out into the moment and connecting me with everyone I loved." David picked up the bottle of saki and topped up his glass. "Soy sauce sure makes me thirsty," he smiled.

"Where was I? Starting with the members of my family, I saw each one of them stop whatever it was they were doing in that moment and turn and smile and let me know that they loved me. It was a simple acknowledgement but the consequences were profound. This connection with and gratitude for those who loved me, rippled out through space and time. Moving backwards through my life, even the most insignificant interactions with strangers where love had been shared, was shown to me. I soon realized that I had opened the book of my life, the *akashic records*; the storehouse called my subconscious. I thought that this must be the 'life flashing before my eyes', of which people who have near death experiences, speak.

Angie nodded to herself. *I too had a similar experience*, she thought.

"I think I'll put the last of the sushi in the fridge to stop it spoiling, if you've had enough?" enquired David.

"Sure. Good idea," replied Angie without opening her eyes. Angie felt connected with David's experience and knew they had shared a similar awakening. She heard him return and sit down on the floor again.

"So anyway, connected to each thought were little tests of my ability to recognize their meaning and understand their message. Each time I relayed to my mind that I understood, it was as though a little cheer would erupt. Curious, who is witnessing these thoughts, I thought? Immediately a new wave of energy coursed through my being. It was as though all those who loved me were taking this journey with me and encouraging me along the way.

The energy continued to flow, and more images and understanding came. As each chakra was stimulated and encouraged to blossom a little more, my consciousness was taken to new levels and into new realms of knowledge and experience. My physiology was lighting up like a Christmas tree and my senses were heightened as they never had been before. My ears popped and I could suddenly hear everything around me with new and greater clarity. All the sibilance of the waves caressing the pebbles at my feet, added another level of tingling to my being.

My eyes seemed to come truly into focus. Not only could I see prana dancing but now I could make out the web they were dancing on. It was as though I could see the very fabric of creation. Air, which I had always thought of as fundamentally empty, was now full of substance, it had a density I could perceive and I was aware that I was a denser part of the same fabric.

The images I could see in my mind's eye and the realizations I was having about the nature of my existence were intimately interwoven, each affecting the other. My internal imaging had been taking me on a journey through my life; through all the beauty and richness of a life I had essentially taken for granted most of the time. Back through my teenage years at school and hanging out with friends and family. Back through adolescence and childhood, images of a happy child, a life blessed with opportunity and love; the richest life one could ever hope for. All the memories were filled with love, there were no sad or lonely memories. No memories of fear or hate or despair. I knew that in a world of love those memories didn't exist, they couldn't exist. My heart chakra blossomed! In a world of love, even the idea of pain, suffering, misery, hate, loneliness and despair could not exist.

In the part of my mind that was having the running commentary with my deeper-self I was asked if I was willing to trust and to let go. If I went one step further the self that I had associated as me, my ego-self was dead, it simply could not exist. I accepted and the web I saw around me shimmered with this comprehension and the next thing I knew I was literally stepping through a gateway into a larger dimension of consciousness."

Angie opened her eyes and looked at David. She could see a smoldering truth in his eyes. "I am so glad to hear you speak of this. I need to go to the washroom. Back in a second." She stood, straightened her dress and walked gracefully through the kitchenette to the hall beyond, turned right and entered the bathroom. Turning on the light she looked into the mirror and saw the same glow in her own eyes. *"This is real and very intense. Where are we going with this? Just chill. We don't know each other, we're simply going to chat about our crazy experiences. Let's just see what happens."*

Angie took a few deep breaths before walking back to the bay window and sitting in one of the large chairs. "Sorry my knees aren't great for long periods of kneeling, too much gymnastics as a kid I think. Please continue, you had just stepped through a gateway," she giggled.

"Yeah, crazy. I will refer to this higher dimension with many names but one of my favourites is hyperspace, and the reason for this is that unlike the other words I could and do use, this one doesn't have as many cultural misunderstandings. I should therefore be able to paint a better picture of this infinitely complex dimensional continuum and our relationship to it, without affecting too many predetermined mental and emotional associations. Hyperspace; wow what a place!" David stood, slowly bent forward at the hips, rubbed his knees and then sat back in the other chair.

"So there I was faced with my ego death. The realization that if I was to proceed, I, the only me I had ever known, could not come. However, in light of everything I was experiencing, I knew I was loved and there was nothing to fear, not even the immanent dissolution of 'me'. So I smiled and continued. I had thought things were intense before, what a misunderstanding! As soon as I stepped over the threshold everything lit up. My chanting had cleared my throat chakra, my third eye was seeing clearly and had been imaging my inner journey. My chakras were all functioning fully. My kundalini had risen to the top of my head and the thousand petaled lotus of illumination had blossomed. I was connected to my world, my family and all the people I had ever known and who had ever interacted with me with love and compassion. Energy was flowing through my meridians and also through my body, like a strong wind through a screen door.

My love for life and humanity, for all creatures and the Earth itself, was rippling outward to connect with it all. This ripple of love spread around the world and the whole world rejoiced with me. We had arrived. This was the day we had been waiting for the whole of history. We were waking up finally, coming home to ourselves as fully Divine Beings. This was Christ's' second coming, and it was every one of us realizing our true nature. That we are Love.

The joy and bliss and ecstasy of this moment of Spiritual birth is beyond all the metaphors and adjectives at my disposal. Quite simply ineffable. There I was, intimately connected to every living being on the planet, and the whole world was one communicating intelligence. Everybody was aware of their connection to everyone and everything. We were all one consciousness, an awareness and experience of pure love; Divine beings. In my mind's eye everyone was dancing and rejoicing, guns were turned into plough-shares, sworn enemies were embracing and remembering that they were brothers in this beautiful dance of creation. The Golden Age was born and we were the blessed to be alive and to experience it!"

So much had transpired in the last four weeks Angie could hardly believe she was en route to a destination she had never even heard of until only hours before she booked her ticket. *I love the serendipity of travel*, she thought, gazing out the window onto the huge expanse of the Himalayan mountain range to her right, as they flew towards Delhi airport.

She turned towards Shala as the credits began to roll on the in-flight movie Shala had been watching, and placing her hand on her forearm, gave it a little squeeze. Shala turned her head and smiled at Angie, the excitement of their adventure blazing from her dark brown eyes. *What a beautiful mix of ethnicities*, thought Angie, before giving Shala another squeeze and turning back to the window to look at the amazing landscape below. After a while Angie closed her eyes and thought back to that first weekend with David and again recalled him describing more of his transcendental experience by the lake, as they sat for hours in the overstuffed lounge chairs in his downtown suite.

"My awareness and experience was of the infinitely dense vibrating continuum of conscious space-time. Every atom is connected to and aware of every other atom in the ocean of creation and it is all pulsing with an indescribable magnitude of power. Becoming a microcosm of the whole system happens when we dissolve the notion of boundaries separating us from the whole system. When those boundary definitions are in place we generate false observations of reality; we think we are separate. We are not separate from the whole system, we just believe we are. Feeling literally as though you are the planet Earth flying through space, because you no longer identify with your old view of self being limited by your skin, is like traveling from the back roads of consciousness onto the superhighway of information processing.

What had previously been thought processes, feelings and imagery at a heightened state of awareness was now almost banal. I had access to every piece of information ever recorded and it was being updated every instant by every quantum nodal point in the entire system. I was the jewel glittering in hyperspace. Creation is an information field. All the information recorded in my lifetime not only by my body-mind but all the information recorded by every living creature is contained within the field. Our bodies are the technology for recording the data and the hard drive storage unit; a living library of a journey of three billion years of biological evolution. Our entire Earth history was there for me to see and feel. Out of all the probable outcomes, out of the almost infinite improbability of existence, here we are!

The waves of intelligence, love and wisdom kept flowing, both up from within me and in from without. The energy moved in a way that can only be described by an understanding of hyperspace; a topographically infinite structure of surface membranes. As I breathed with the rhythm of the waves on the lake, I became more aware of the forces acting on the planet. I could feel these energies in relation to another new frontier of experience; Space. As I focused my attention on the forces pulling on the planet, the waves coming up from within also surged with more power. I was going to another level". Angie recalled how David had looked at her with an expression of pure wonder in that moment.

"There I was experiencing oneness with the whole planet, thinking life couldn't possibly get any better than this, when my consciousness started moving again. I was looking out towards the horizon, aware of the sun just above my line of sight, when a moment I shared with my friend in her pyramid the previous year popped into my thoughts. It was a night we shared talking and listening to the composer Philip Glass. His opera Akhenaten had the line '...*open are the double doors of the horizon, unlocked are its bolts*' spoken in a beautiful rich resonant voice. The passage was an adaptation from an ancient Egyptian ritual and for me it meant 'you now have access to your full cortical function.' The 'double doors of the horizon' were the two hemispheres of my brain, and they were open for business!

Whole brain processing is not the schizophrenic, ambiguous experience of normal waking consciousness, where your thoughts move from one hemisphere to the other. Whole brain processing has the qualities of both hemispheres unified into a cohesive unit. Left brain, logical sequential processing is expanded by right brain non-local, non-spatial, everywhere and everywhen processing. The experience of being totally present and intimately connected to every other moment shaping this moment. We are a product of the past; the entire past. Every single event in the universe has had an influence on our existence, from the big bang to the present moment". Angie stopped the playback of David's talk and pondered these ideas for a while trying to embody what he was saying. She mentally expanded her own internal imagining to incorporate herself on the plane as it flew towards Delhi with the enormity of the Himalayas stretching over the landscape below.

After a while of connecting with her present moment she went back to listening to David. "As I mentioned previously, I had already traversed DNA's winding history, for it was all recorded, and I was its living testament. Morphology is the shape of consciousness. Like Goethe said, 'geometry is frozen music'. The gnomic structure of our brain contains previous growths of biological development from the simplest organisms, through reptiles, mammals and on up to humans. At the apex of this long unbroken journey sat me. I was pulsing with life-force. It was like being one hundred percent alive. The journey of this new expanded self now headed in several directions at once. I simultaneously went inwards, upwards, backwards and forwards.

The inward journey was into my body and down to the cellular level. The upward journey was out into space above the Earth and on towards the sun. The backwards journey was beyond the formation of DNA on Earth and the forwards journey was into our immanent and probable future. I also deepened my feelings of oneness with the planet as it flew through space. What a ride! Better than the best amusement park ride, that's for certain. Being plugged into the Divine intelligence of Mother Earth is indescribable bliss and joy and ecstasy!"

David had then opened his eyes and looked at Angie. "How are you doing? Can I get you anything? Are you comfortable? I feel bad doing all the talking," he said, as he picked up his glass of mineral water and took another sip. "That saki made me overly garrulous".

"No. Please, you are speaking words that are a balm to my troubled soul. I will share with you my last two weeks, but first I would like you to continue until you have completed your story. Trust me, I am enjoying it on many levels," she replied looking deeply into his eyes.

David took a deep breath and continued. "OK. Stop me if I get too carried away. I'll take the inward journey first, although they are all intimately related and were occurring simultaneously".

"In my mind I went down into a cell and looked at my DNA structure, and saw dormant codes, possible future instructions of forms we could become as well as my phylogeny. I also intuited that the DNA spiral acted like a mini transceiver tuning into an information spectrum much like a TV antenna tuning into radio waves. Operating on a very high frequency I could sense my cells receiving instructions from this field in order for my cells to know how to differentiate. Every cell was buzzing lie and iron filing held in a magnetic field. The power of biology life is incredible.

I took my awareness through the molecules of the proteins and down into the atoms. I kept accelerating as I went down into a single atom and then through into the nucleus, racing faster and faster, sensing the protons and neutrons enlarge behind me. Then between the spaces of the protons and neutrons down and down I went and as I was getting further and further away from matter - the points represented by subatomic nodes of vibrating energy - I was heading deeper into space. I know this sounds completely illogical but space is infinite inside as well. I was heading into what Taoists call the Void, but it's not the nothing we in the West hypothesize. Quantum theory now assumes that all of space is a field effect and interprets particles as excitations of this field, which is a much closer model to what I experienced."

David paused and took another sip of mineral water and Angie decided to as well.

"This is a bit technical, but the empty vacuum of old-school physics is today replaced by an active medium in which virtual particles come into and go out of existence on timescales allowed by Heisenberg's uncertainty principle. A concrete proof of this is the measurement of the distance or energy dependence of the fine-structure constant. This is explained by vacuum polarization, whereby the electric charge of a real particle is partially screened by those of other virtual particles. Dark energy is a term I'm sure you've heard thrown around lately?"

"Yes. So if I understand you correctly, what you are saying is, in the darkness of space, quantum particles are points of vibrating energy arising spontaneously out of the field effect of space as a medium of substance and these particles can be measured by the effects of other phantom particles?" asked Angie, eyes still closed as she visualized David's description, "and all of creation is built of this vibrating stuff as it were; an ocean of energy in the same way we have an ocean of salty water."

"Precisely. We think of ourselves, or any piece of matter, as separate from this ocean but we are immersed in the ocean the same as every drop of water or atom of hydrogen and oxygen in the literal sea."

"Yes, this is exactly how I feel it. Please go on," finished Angie, a smile on her face. David took a moment to drink in her beauty and then continued.

"Outwardly my consciousness rose up into the sky, gaining perspective of my body sitting on the edge of the lake in the highlands of Switzerland. Up and up, as if I was ascending in a hot air balloon. I saw the ground falling away as I went higher and higher and the mountains receded and the lake became a pale blue splash in a landscape of green and brown and white. Up and up until I was looking down on Earth as if from a satellite and then, turning my attention towards the sky, I raced into the Sun. However, the sun was not a nuclear furnace but a massive Divine Being. I won't even try and describe the enormity of its presence.

Once through the Sun I was on a Stargate ride racing through portals. Penetration with the portals coincided with the awakening of more chakras above my crown chakra. As I mentioned previously, I had no idea there even existed more chakras but here I was activating them and then passing through them. As I passed through each one it coincided with moving through what seemed to be other suns of other solar systems and other planes of existence. The journey had a distinct destination but I had no idea where that might be, but intuited it was momentous. The bliss kept increasing, the planet kept rejoicing and I kept expanding. Whoosh, another portal, access to more information, but I wasn't stopping to explore. I knew each chakra was a doorway to rediscovering innate powers of healing and accessing long lost dimensional histories but this didn't matter, I was on a mission. I was going to the end. No matter what, I was going to the end".

Angie opened her eyes slightly and looked out the window for a while, letting the infinite blue sky wash over her.

"Backwards into the past, I went beyond the creation of DNA. I went to the formation of Earth, the rocks and the minerals and crystals, all the elements of Earth. I saw the Earth coalesce out of the space dust and other debris of the early solar system. I continued racing backwards, faster and faster through cosmic history. The Universe was unwinding to its simplest form. Back to the beginning, which was just a pause in the cycle of universes breathing in and breathing out. It seemed like the only difference between a quantum particle blinking into and winking out of existence and a universe doing the same thing is the amount of memory it requires.

Forward was like a combination of the other three and they were all aspects of each other. Forwards is where the limitless future awaits us. As K.C. Cole says; *Potential, it turns out, is one of the most impressive properties of nothing.* In an instant, like the final push in the birth of a newborn baby, I arrived. Shooting through all directions in one final culminating involution, I completed the loop. The final portal was the black-hole at the centre of our galaxy. I was through in all directions. Inward, outward, backward and forward were all aspects of me finding and merging with the whole. When I burst through the final chakra at the top of the column it was the ultimate crown. I had flown through the centre of our galaxy, through the black hole, out of which all energy and matter in our galaxy has come. I was united with Universal Mind, Infinite Space, the Source of all there Is; the endless sea of Pure Consciousness.

There was nowhere left to go. I had traversed all of space in every direction and it all led to the same place: Here and Now. The most exquisite thing was I still had a body. I was still incarnate and that was the ultimate prize. The message from every aspect of my being, from my literal brothers and sisters on Earth to my metaphysical brothers and sisters of all other dimensions, all our ancestors and all the other incarnations we have all had, from beings on other planets in other solar systems of our galaxy to beings in other dimensions of the hologram, was a message of completion and Love. We had arrived. Spirit was made flesh and flesh was pure energy. I was the infinite universe experiencing itself. My body was vibrating pure love energy, an interference pattern generated from the interaction of cosmic waves of improbability. A dream of infinite complexity and pure simplicity and it was all One. As I sat there for the next few hours, I was able to travel through each of my chakras and discover their hidden realms and secret knowledge, but the overall experience was the *Fractal Edge of Universal Mind* an infinite enfolded topology of evolving consciousness."

"Water?" inquired the flight attendant and Angie opened her eyes coming back to the present.

"Yes, please," she replied and passed her little plastic cup to Shala to hold while the attendant poured the water. *Thank you,* she mouthed, as the woman looked briefly at her and smiled. They were traveling with Air India, having changed planes in Taiwan and Angie loved their outfits. She couldn't think of them as a uniform. *The colours and patterns are too vibrant and exquisite,* she thought. *Even before my experience their clothes would be intense*, she observed, as another attendant moved past up the aisle.

Shala had taken off her headphones and was arranging the small inflight pillows on the foldout tray table attached to the back of the seat in front of her, so she could rest her head and try for a little more sleep before they landed. "I'm excited and quite exhausted. An hour nap and then we should start our decent into Delhi. Did you sleep much during the night?" asked Shala, with her head lying sideways on the pile of pillows, one eye closed and the other looking past Angie and out the cabin window into the early morning blue sky.

"Yeah, it wasn't too bad. As you know my memory recall is very good lately so I am able to recite long pieces of the sacred Hindu texts I am studying. I do that until my mind feels sufficiently taxed and then I visualize golden light slowly filling me up like a glass of lemonade, and I usually fall sleep before I'm full," laughed Angie.

"That sounds neat. I'm going to try it now," replied Shala and closed her eye. "See you soon my friend."

"Peaceful sleep to you," said Angie, as she pulled the blanket up around Shala's shoulders. Lowering the window covering she too closed her eyes. Angie pictured herself filling up with liquid light and then continued on with her memories of her afternoon with David.

After David had finished describing his experience by the lake, Angie had shared her experience at the rivers' edge and the activation of her chakras later that evening with Archer. They then discussed different theories and some ideas for sharing their experiences with a larger audience. Later she asked him if he could go through the salient points of his book and explain to her what he believed was going on at the deeper levels.

David was very excited to hear of Angie's kundalini awakening, and shared his thoughts on the biological and quantum electrochemical push for the spontaneous unfolding that was happening to more and more individuals. According to David, evolution was at work within humans, but it was not the morphology of biology that was evolving, it was consciousness. Electromagnetic energy, oscillating and harmonizing with galactic resonance, on the subtle levels of what defined a human being. Galactic frequencies of electromagnetic radiation were, somehow exciting dormant and blocked energy centers within the human body, using the network of meridians the Chinese had been working with for centuries.

Angie liked that he didn't get unnecessarily emotional describing his ideas and how he kept them grounded in measurable phenomena. The peace and truth of his convictions was evident in his voice and demeanour; calm and soothing. His European accent was delightful too.

In her mind's eye she went back to the moment where he summarized part of his book for her. "In chapter three I discuss holograms and fractals as a metaphor for describing what physicist David Bohm calls the implicate and explicate order. His views have had a great influence on mine as he draws from the ancient Taoist ideas of the Void. Do you know how a hologram works?" he asked, as he poured more mineral water for himself and topped up her glass also.

"I remember going to a science fair with my family when I was about twelve and one of the displays was a series of holograms. I was fascinated but had no idea how they were created. I recall walking around the hologram and being impressed, able to see the scene from behind. I remember thinking it's like how the eyes in some paintings will follow you. I'm happy to hear about holograms again," she replied as she watched the glass filling with the slightly effervescent liquid.

"Cool. Well, a hologram is a 3D image made with the aid of lasers. To make a hologram, the object to be reproduced is first bathed in the light of a laser beam. Then a second laser beam is aimed at the reflected light of the first laser and the resulting interference pattern generates the hologram. You would have seen this done on film also. It looks like a meaningless swirl of light and dark lines until the developed film is illuminated by another laser beam, then a three-dimensional image of the original object appears. They are on most currency these days for security reasons and on artworks, even on novelty items. These however only need visible light reflected off the silver backing to generate the hologram.

The three-dimensionality of such images is not the only characteristic of a hologram. If the film of a hologram, say an apple for instance, is cut in half and then illuminated by a laser, each half will still be found to contain the entire image of the apple. Even if the halves are divided again, each piece of film will always be found to contain a smaller but complete version of the original image. Unlike normal photographs, every part of a hologram contains all the information possessed by the whole. The whole in every part nature of a hologram and the self-similarity of fractals throughout their infinite scale provides us with an entirely new way of understanding organization and order."

David let Angie ponder for several minutes what he had discussed before he continued.

"Resonance is the key to merging with the totality of existence. A lot of work has been done studying the effects of coherent emotion. Coherent emotion is equivalent to laser light. Researchers have amassed reams of data relating to the idea that we can, through focused intent, change neurological activity and therefore consciousness, by feeling particular emotional states. This is primarily achieved by focusing on the feelings of love, compassion and peace. Although the idea of love may seem unscientific it turns out that we can measure specific frequencies which relate directly to the test subjects' emotive capacity. We can also measure changes in the electrical activity of the brain, thereby giving us an excellent correlation between emotion and consciousness.

The heart's beat provides a very dramatic picture on an EKG at the moment of love. The specific EKG frequency cascade which correlates directly with the feeling of love, experienced cross-culturally, is the golden ratio also known as the phi ratio. Plotted on an oscillograph, this specific heartbeat pattern shows how the voltage drops at the cascade frequency ratio of the Fibonacci sequence. This heart-beat pulse has astounding brainwave coherence and resonance. The energy field that emanates from the heart is measurable and recordable and has shown to generate activity in both hemispheres of the cerebellum, whereby the temporal lobes can be seen to operate together. Whole brain processing enriches brain functioning to a superior level of heightened awareness."

Angie opened her eyes when the pilot announced their descent into Delhi airport as the last of what David had been describing made its way to her conscious mind. "The physiological heart is more than the mechanical pump our grandfathers believed. As researchers have said 'the heart is a nest of simple torus shaped field effects, whose symmetry permits pressure to share space. In our unified field, the inertia of coherence which occurs when spin is stored is what we call matter'. In other words, when we analyze the seven layers of muscle and how they squeeze in sequence to move the blood around the body, we see a wave-guide of Golden Mean proportions. Just as the electrical graph of EKG showed a beat node of phi proportions, so too does the muscular contractions of the heart during its experience of love."

Angie thought of how many ideas she needed to digest and more of their conversation she wanted to bring to awareness over the next few weeks. Smiling, she turned to watch Shala who still slept, evidenced by a small string of saliva hanging from her parted lips onto the small in-flight pillow. Angie rubbed the back of her neck and turned and looked out the window into a smog obliterating much of the landscape below.

Chapter Five - Back to the Future

Katelyn stumbled backwards with a grunt, tripped and pulled the woman over the railing and down on top of her. For the briefest of moments the two of them looked into each other's eyes and both felt they were looking at a sister or close relation. Katelyn thought of her first cousin who so closely resembled this woman.

The woman stood and pulled Katelyn to her feet, then dusted herself off. Reaching her hands to her face she rubbed dust out of the corner of her eyes with the tips of her little fingers, yawned, equalizing the pressure in her ears, briefly looked into Katelyn's eyes again, then down to the glowing spiral on her chest. Katelyn looked past the woman into the vortex then back at the woman. "Sorry but I am in shock. Who are you? When did you go into the vortex?" Taking a closer look at her clothes Katelyn realized she must be a local woman. "Do you speak English?", asking louder than was necessary.

"Very little," replied the woman, before tears of joy and great sobs wracked her lithe frame. "I made it back," she hollered in her native tongue and reached out and embraced

Katelyn tightly, tears streaming down her face. "I made it back!"

Katelyn raised her left arm, looked at her watch and saw her half hour was over. "Please you must come with me," she whispered in the woman's ear. Extricating herself from the woman's embrace and taking her hand, she lead her back through the opening, out onto the mountains' side and into the sunshine. The woman closed her eyes and turned her face to the morning's soft and warming luminescence, a huge smile spreading across her sunlit face. The next person in line for the portal experience, a male named Richard from Ireland who had been chatting with Katelyn as they waited in line, smiled as he approached. Katelyn smiled back and moved out of the way so he could pass on the narrow path.

Richard was about to ask Katelyn about her experience but saw the woman and asked, "Where did she come from?" a puzzled look forming at the corner of his eyes, his brow furrowing as realization plied in on his thoughts, and before Katelyn could reply he blurted, "What in the world, she's come out of the portal. No way, that's crazy! I've heard stories but this; whoa. Anyway, my turn. See you back at camp." Moving past them he disappeared through the opening.

Katelyn looked at the woman standing there with her eyes closed, palms together in front of her heart, a radiant smile outshining the sun, and lightly took hold of her left elbow. "We should be getting down to the village. I think we need to go and see Gwylin." At the mention of Gwylin's name the woman opened her eyes and nodded her head. "Gwylin," she gasped, reached down to a rich tapestry bag at her side, then moved past Katelyn and lead the way down the winding path to the base of the mountain. As they passed each of the checkpoints, the morning visitors would stop chatting and stare at the woman, who simply smiled in return. Katelyn felt like royalty as she and her doppelganger made their way past the lineup. The feelings from the proximity to the portal had waned considerably but Katelyn still felt euphoric.

Hand in hand they made their way across the valley floor and along a track Katelyn hadn't seen before, which headed slightly up the valley before turning onto a narrow meadow between the river and the base of the mountain. Small yellow petalled flowers with bright purple stamen were swaying slightly in the light morning breeze and seemed to be smiling up at her. Katelyn wanted to stop and lay down but the woman gestured she must get to the camp as soon as possible, so they continued on down to the river. They crossed a narrow bridge made from hand-hewn wooden planks, then wound their way downstream to the clearing and the group of huts Katelyn had left only two hours ago. *It feels like a lifetime since I was here,* she thought, as a holler went out from one of the boys as he approached them on his way to the river. Several other boys came running over to them followed by a group of women with Gwylin in the lead. More precisely, they came to the woman who had emerged from the portal. Katelyn could see the absolute amazement on the faces of the local people. *Who is she and how long has she been gone?* she wondered.

Gwylin turned to Katelyn eyes wide and twinkling, exclaiming: "This is my sister, Naldi!" before taking both their hands and leading them to the small hut where Katelyn spent the previous night. "Please stay outside for a little while but do not leave. Sorry, this is very momentous occasion for my people," said Gwylin, as she turned and led her sister inside.

Katelyn walked over to the fire-pit, sat on a log, closed her eyes and reflected on her experience at the portal, then recalled what Gwylin had just said. *"What? Naldi is Gwylin's sister. She must mean sister as in spiritual sister, like a nun or something."* She unconsciously lifted her left hand to the fossilized pendant and held it tightly.

Anthony was washing his breakfast utensils and deciding what to do about finding Katelyn. He knew she had an 8:00 am rendezvous with the portal and that he could have met her at the base of the trail up the mountain if he really felt it necessary to confirm she was okay. He decided to wait until lunch time before searching for her. *Give her some space and trust in her unfolding path, she'll be fine,* he concluded.

He dried his kit, placed it back in his pack and headed out of the hall towards their tent. His curiosity had grown considerably this morning after listening to more pilgrims discussing their experiences from yesterday. *Is this designed to test my faith or open me up to the greater mysteries of God's infinite creation?,* he pondered, as he looked at the mountain looming magnificent before him in the morning sun. *What would Jesus do?,* he thought, but was distracted by a group of yelling boys as they raced past him towards the town. There was an extra level of seriousness he noticed on the faces of the little hooligans. *What's going on?,* he wondered, as he continued towards the path that lead to his tent. He had walked about twenty-five yards up the path to the campsite when the group of boys went racing by again, only this time they were followed by a line of what seemed like most of the locals from town. Twenty or thirty of the shopkeepers and their assistants were making their way hastily up river. *Curious?* he thought and continued to his tent. After stowing his breakfast gear he packed some energy bars and headed into town.

Anthony went to enter the rental shop to hire another bike for the morning but the door was locked. He turned and looked across the street to the other rental shop and it too was closed. He looked at the camping supply store next door and it was closed. A few other tourists were walking towards him from the other end of town and he called out to them "Where is everybody?"

"We were going to ask you the same question. We just got off the bus and everything is closed. We were told a porter would meet us and take us to the orientation hut, where-ever that is?" said a dark haired man in his late twenties with a South American accent.

"I know, follow me." Anthony led them back up the street, turned the first corner to the right and stood in front of the closed orientation building. "Davo will know what's going on. Sorry, follow me." Arriving at Davo's little shop he was glad to see the door was open, entering, he took off his sunglasses and called out Davo's name.

"Out the back man", came the response as Anthony led the newcomers through the store and out onto the back deck where they found Davo with a beer and a cigarette in one hand and a pail of glue in the other. He took a long pull on his can of beer, then swallowing, he crushed the can and threw it into a pile off in the corner, put the cigarette to his lips and took a drag, then placed it on the edge of the wooden bench which had one of his upturned rafts laying on it, and started slathering glue in an area marked with white chalk.

"What's goin' on man?" he asked, testing the glue's tackiness with the piece of wood he used to apply it.

"Any idea where all the townsfolk have gone?" asked Anthony, enjoying the easy-going Aussie's demeanour. *I don't think he'd even worry if his pants were on fire,* he smiled to himself.

"Shops are all closed are they?" asked Davo as he worked a red rubber patch into place. Intuiting that was exactly the case he continued, "Religious festival, death, birth, return of a mountain goat, who knows mate. Any number of reasons with these guys. Whaddaya need?

"Nothing really, I was going to rent a bike and go for a ride and these guys just arrived and were hoping to get the low down at orientation," replied Anthony as casually as he could muster.

"Oh yeah, no problem, simple. You can borrow my bike," Davo indicated with a slight nod of his head to the right, where Anthony saw an expensive mountain bike propped up against the fence. Davo tested the rubber patch for full adhesion and said, "Just bring her back in one piece. I'll take these guys down to the mess hall." Davo took a long draw on his cigarette before knocking off the burning ember and the placed the butt behind his ear.

"Davo's my name, where you guys from?" he asked, and ushered them back through his shop and out into the street, closing the door behind him. Anthony grabbed the bike, wheeled it through the gate and met them around the front as they headed back out of town towards the mess hall.

"Hey thanks Davo, I really appreciate the loan of the bike. I'll be back in a couple of hours," Anthony said, as he headed off in the direction of the previous day's trails.

"No worries mate, enjoy. Turning to the group Davo continued, "So your name's Holly, you're from Amsterdam. Your name's Mary, you're from Liverpool. Your name's Pedro, you're from Brazil, you're Enrique also from Brazil and your name's Michaela from Czechoslovakia." They all nodded and smiled. "So who's coming white water-rafting with me this afternoon? Package deal if you all come together, how's that sound, best rapids in the world up here. Beautiful scenery too. So who's first into the portal?" he finished, having planted the seed of his sales pitch.

"We were hoping you could tell us," said Pedro, as they left the final row of shops and started along the trail towards the hall.

"Oh yeah, no orientation yet. How many other pilgrims on the bus with you?" asked Davo, looking at Mary, since he figured her English should be the best.

"Aght lest firty of ous, but we were last to git our kit, the others all wandered orf 'round toon when no-one cam for us," she replied in her thick Liverpool accent. Davo thought it would be easier to understand someone who spoke English as their second language.

"No matter. It's not like they're going anywhere. Probably smelled the coffee up at Ramesh's cafe, he'll be open. Seems like only the locals have closed shop. I'm curious to find out what's goin' on though," he said, pulling the cigarette from behind his ear and re-lighting it.

They strode along the well-trodden path for a few more minutes discussing the possibilities and arrived at the mess hall, as two pilgrims came hurriedly from the direction of the mountain, and in between catching their breath, told them that a woman had come out of the portal that morning.

"Un-bloody-likely," said Davo "but you never know, they've been sending them in there for hundreds of years, it's probably full on the other side," laughing at his own joke. The two messengers didn't think it was very funny and relayed how they had been standing in line when the woman came past them. At that point Richard came out of the mess hall and said, "It's true man. I was the next one to go in and the girl who went before me came out with the woman. Apparently they're both over at the shaman's campsite.

"Well, that explains why the shops are all shut then. The return of one of their nag pa. Things are going to get decidedly more interesting around here now. They have been waiting for a nag pa to return for over two hundred generations." Davo took one final drag on his cigarette, extinguished the burning ember between his thumb and forefinger and flicked the butt to the ground as Michaela asked, "What's a nag pa?".

"A nag pa is one of the chosen ones with highly refined 'magical powers'," replied Davo emphasizing the last part with finger quotations, to illustrate his appraisal of the idea. They all turned to watch what seemed to be the rest of the group from this morning's bus amble towards them.

Raising his voice as the others arrived, Davo said "The deal seems to be that something very special has happened for the locals and as such they have closed-up shop; possibly for the rest of the day. Normally you would attend an orientation meeting, be allocated campsites and visitation times for the portal. Today is going to be 'entertain yourself until further notice' day. I will be hitting the rapids this afternoon and I can take ten of you. First in, best dressed as they say. Meanwhile have something to eat or go find yourself a campsite, which are up the path to the right on your way back into town. I'm going to hang out here for about half an hour acting as an information stand if you have any questions. The price is one cigarette for every question satisfactorily answered!"

Turning to Richard, Davo asked: "So how old did this woman look?"

"Do you know the girl Katelyn?" Davo nodded, "Well she looks like she could be her twin sister," said Richard, eyes wide.

"Yeah, see, that's where my BS meter starts going into the red because the last time they sent anyone in there was about fifty years ago. Well, time will tell and of course there is no way for us to know for sure if it's true. Could be a woman from another village come to bring the myth to life as it were. Entice even more tourists, if you get my drift. You also mentioned Katelyn's at their campsite, which doesn't sound right to me. They don't like foreigners going anywhere near there." Davo turned to Michaela and asked: "You want to try white-water rafting this afternoon sweetheart?"

Michaela smiled but shook her head no. "I want to go to the portal as soon as possible. When can we get our times allocated?"

"Well, that will depend on when the villagers decide. If it's true that one of their chosen ones has returned, they might just close the whole operation down for all I know," said Davo, frowning at the idea; his business would be finished if that were the case.

"Half price for the ten who want to come white-water rafting with me this afternoon. River is perfect, weather is perfect. Arms raised to the sky, Davo, imitating The Joker from Batman, called out, "It don't get any better than this folks!"

Katelyn held the fossil in her right hand, remembering the patterns and feelings from her time at the portal. *I have to get back there. I wonder what's going to happen now Naldi has returned? Gwylin said I am needed, that they have been waiting for me. I wonder what she meant? I wonder if she still thinks the same way now? Probably was their desperate attempt to fulfill their ancient prophecy. Where in the world has Naldi been?*

There was a shout from behind her and she turned to see Gwylin and Naldi standing facing each other in front of the hut, holding what seemed to be a small human skull between them. The wolf head emerged from the animal hide flap of the hut, with it's human wearer slinking on all fours around the two of them, sniffing and howling as he went.

Children were running crazily in every direction, yelling as the shopkeepers from town arrived. Taking one look at Naldi they too started howling, whooping, jumping up and down and running around like the children.

Katelyn stood and started to make her way towards Naldi, but Gwylin shook her head, so she stopped. The wolfman approached Katelyn, and snarling, leapt and tore the pendant from around her neck, the leather thong biting into her flesh before snapping. With a stab of pain and feeling of loss, she started to cry. She put her hands to her face and sobbed. *This is not what I signed up for,* a wave of sadness washing over her. Noticing the silence, she gathered herself, wiped the last of her tears away and opened her eyes. Standing directly in front of her was Naldi holding the large skull-shaped object out to her, with a gentle smile on her face. *What in the world is going on now?* she thought, but did not move to take the proffered idol.

Gwylin, who she hadn't noticed standing at her side, pinched her thigh and lifted Katelyn's left arm up towards the skull. "What is going on Gwylin, I can't take this, it's all too much."

Gwylin hissed, "Shhh miss, this is your destiny you are a chosen one like Naldi. You have work to do at the portal, take the power stone. Today we feast and tomorrow…" She was cut off by the wolfman's howl of impatience, so Katelyn took the stone, and again the villagers went wild, whooping and hollering and shaking, like a people possessed.

For Angie and Shala the journey from Delhi to Tang Ting had been an extremely uncomfortable ride in an overfilled bus, but the conversations had been interesting; nearly everyone on board was heading to their personal encounter with the portal. However, after arriving they were very disconcerted to be wandering around with a group of other pilgrims with no idea what was going on.

Angie turned to Shala as Davo finished his sales pitch offering half price white-water rafting, and asked her: "Shall we get a campsite first and then come back here and make some lunch?"

"Sounds perfect. I'm tired, hungry and confused. What did he mean, they may just close the whole operation down? He can't be serious, do you think? I need to lie down," replied Shala, as dejected and tired looking as Angie had ever seen her.

Turning and heading back towards the turnoff to the campsite, Angie thought about what she could say to lift Shala's spirits, but felt the enormity of not knowing what was going to happen too much for her to reconcile. Finally, looking around at the skyline she said "This is not unlike hiking in the Rockies. I almost feel at home."

Shala looked around her too and felt better. "You're right Angie, this is good. It's a long way to come to feel at home but it'll do until we find out more. I can't believe we survived that bus ride. A couple times there I really thought we were goners," she laughed, releasing a big ball of pent-up emotion.

"Yes, you're unlikely to survive when your bus plummets from off a thousand foot ledge. Certainly puts life into perspective when you feel you could die every ten minutes. I kept thinking how annoyed I used to get waiting on the bus, stuck in peak-hour traffic on my way to work, and how I would give anything to be safely stuck there again rather than clumping along in the Himalayas with death lurking around every corner. However, now I'm here and the ordeal is done, I feel exhausted but really alive at the same time," said Angie, turning to look at Shala as they rounded the corner onto the trail to the campsites.

Shala had been quiet as they continued up the track, then finally responded saying, "I know what you mean, my mind is really clear. How about this spot?" she asked, surveying a little area of short grass on which to pitch their tent.

"To be honest, I think anywhere is going to be awesome. It's so beautiful here. You could never describe this to anyone. It's like home but it's not. The energy here is different. These mountains feel different. The lighting is different." Closing her eyes and dropping her pack to the ground, Angie lifted her arms to the sky and let out a huge "Yahoo," and then took several deep breaths. Shala did the same, and finishing, they looked into each other's eyes and started laughing.

"I'll set the tent if you want to blow up the thermorests and get the sleeping bags ready," said Angie as she knelt to the ground and started removing the tent poles and ground sheet from the tent bag.

"No worries missy," came Shala's reply. "And then we nap!"

Once they were settled into their sleeping bags Shala fell straight to sleep. Angie however wanted to meditate as she found it far more restful than a short sleep. She pictured herself standing at the top of a stone staircase of one hundred steps. Descending the staircase one step at a time she started counting backwards from 100. The trick was to keep focused and to not drift off thinking other thoughts. Ninety-nine, ninety-eight, ninety-seven… step by step, down and down. The stone staircase was cut aeons ago by unknown hands with bright light from flaming sconces, held in place by especially designed iron braces mounted onto the rough hewn rock walls.

Down and down she stepped, her breathing strong and even. Pausing and reflecting every ten stairs, releasing the tension in her body. At the base of the stairs, loomed two huge wooden doors with intricate ironwork in the shape of a massive oak tree. Beyond the doors the realm of her subconscious lay waiting. Pushing open the doors she stepped off the ledge into the blackness of space, her breath catching in her throat as she falls but knows it's a meaningless spatial reference in the infinite blackness. She then realizes she's floating, and crosses her legs to sit in full lotus; the backs of her hands resting on her knees, index finger and thumb forming a circle.

Soon enough a vision begins. Angie sees herself standing with Shala and two women who look like sisters, their brown eyes and long dark hair shining in the light emanating from behind her. She is aware of a powerful presence to her left but can't turn to see it. They are preparing to do something of consequence and the excitement is palpable. The four of them have resolved within themselves that this undertaking is worth the risks involved. One of the women has been through this before and reassures them with a gentle smile. Angie turns to see a kaleidoscope of swirling colours consuming the entire space in front of them as the woman who has made the journey before walks forward and disappears from view. Angie watches as Shala follows the second woman through and then it is her turn. She steps forward but her body starts to vibrate so intensely she is jarred back into the awareness of lying in her tent with Shala snoring by her side.

"Well, if that ain't the Portal of Creation then I'm a monkey's uncle," she whispered to the thin forest-green fabric of their tent. She rolled over onto her side, closed her eyes, and seeing the swirling colours again, drifted off to sleep.

Shala rocked Angie gently awake with her hand on her shoulder. "Hungry my lovely?" she whispered as Angie's eyes fluttered open. "I know I am. Man, that was a good sleep. I went out like a light. Don't even remember dreaming." Pushing her sleeping bag down her legs she knelt, undid the zipper on the tent and crawled outside. "I wonder what time it is?" she asked knowing neither of them wore watches. "I don't think I'm going to be able to tell the time looking at the sun's position up here," she said, pulling her watch out from her backpack before stretching from side to side.

"What do you feel like for lunch, noodles or rice?" she asked, looking up at the mountain behind her, as she leant backwards with her hands on her hips, enjoying the visual counterpoint of land and sky reversed.

"Noodles," came the reply from Angie as she poked her head out of the tent, looked around and soaked up her surroundings. *I wonder if I should tell Shala of my vision or just wait and see what unfolds?* "I'll get the food supplies and utensils, if you want to put all our valuables into one bag."

"Sure Angie," said Shala, as she knelt down and placed a kiss on her forehead. "I feel so much better now. It's really great to be here. I guess it doesn't matter what happens. Destiny is at hand and I trust she is guiding us with wisdom."

"I feel the same way Shala. Let's eat!"

Chapter Six - One Step Beyond

David had just finished the final speaking engagement of his current tour and was patiently signing books, chatting with excited participants after his lecture.

"Yes, it is a curious observation, and recent developments for creating antimatter are having profound effects on our understanding of the moments directly after the Big Bang," he was saying to a group of gentlemen standing to his right, as he signed another book. "The fact that after all the matter and antimatter generated during the Big Bang had interacted, and most of it was annihilated, what we have left fourteen billion years later, is us."

"It is extremely fascinating to contemplate, we truly are made of the stuff of stars," one of the men was saying, "forged in the fiery nuclear furnace of aging suns."

"I know. Once those old suns explode, they send the elements needed to sustain life out into the galaxy to become the building blocks of biology. Incredible!" said another man, as David continued to sign books. "What I'm currently finding interesting are the dark energy and dark matter requirements of the standard model for an accelerating universe…" Although David rarely tired of these conversations, he was longing for the event to end, so he could be with Angie one last time before she flew to India. "…the faster than light speed data coming from the recent experiments on neutrinos is very exciting too".

David was thinking of his time with Angie over the past month and smiling warmly to himself as he looked up and asked the woman in front of him what her name was so he could write it in her copy of his book. "Catherine," she said and continued stating how much she enjoyed his passionate and engaging talk.

"Thank you," he replied, smiling and taking the next book and repeating the task. He glanced at his watch and then looked gratefully at the diminishing line in front of him.

Half an hour later he made his way by taxi to his rented apartment suite where Angie was waiting for him. He opened the door and was greeted by the sound of a Philip Glass opera coming from the stereo in the bedroom. Slipping off his shoes, he walked over to the entrance of the bedroom and watched as Angie twirled in circles, the long piece of light green silk he had given her held between her outstretched hands billowing behind her like a superhero's cape. She wore the hotel's complimentary white silk bathrobe and her hair, still damp from her recent shower, was flinging tiny drops of water into the air around her.

As the piece of music built to a crescendo, Angie leapt onto the king-size bed and extending her arms straight up into the air, twirled as fast as she could until the music abruptly stopped and she crumpled to the bed in a dramatic repose.

She gasped and threw a pillow at David when she finally opened her eyes. "How long have you been there?" she giggled, jumping to her feet as he came running towards her. He dived onto the bed, performing a football tackle but missed her as she leapt sideways and then knelt down on top of him.

"I missed you today," he said, his face pushed into the luxurious bedspread. "Where would you like to go for dinner?"

"You know, I'm thinking tonight I would like to dress up and stay here. Have some take-out delivered and then make love until the sun rises."

David tried to roll over but she pinned him where he was and bit him lightly on the ear. "On second thoughts, I'm going to eat you for dinner," she cooed and bit down harder as he yelped and threw her off him in mock protestation.

"No, I'm going to eat you!" Quick as lightening he grabbed the sash that held her bathrobe closed and pulled it from her. Angie screamed as he swept her feet from under her and, pinning her down with his knee, hog-tied her hands and feet together behind her back.

Angie was laughing too hard to do anything as David tickled the soles of her feet. "No!" she screamed with zero effect. After several minutes of tickling her in various regions he had learned she couldn't tolerate, he untied her, but only after she promised she would not retaliate.

Exhausted, they cuddled for a while and Angie asked him about his day and the final talk he gave. "I bet you're glad it's over."

"I am, but I'm probably going to miss the attention, as silly as that sounds. Also, I have no idea what I am going to do now. You're heading off on a grand adventure and although I have several job opportunities I am reluctant to take a position just yet. I feel I have a role to play in something that isn't yet ready to unfold, but I can't quite put my finger on what it is," he said, as he rolled onto his back and looked at the intricate plaster cornice of acanthus leaves and scrolls, decorating the edge of the bedroom ceiling.

"The timing isn't great but as we discussed before, you can come and find me in India in a few weeks. I just want to help Shala with her journey to the Portal and then back into India. After that I'm free to do whatever I want, which is to be with you," said Angie, as she rolled on top of him and nestled her forehead under his chin.

"I'm really going to miss you Angie," said David, bringing his left hand up and stroking her cheek. Then kissing her on the top of her head he said, "I'll order the food then have a shower while you play dress-ups. How about Sushi again tonight?"

"Sounds good my love," said Angie, as she rolled off him and watched him walk out of the bedroom. "I'm really going to miss you too," she said to the emptiness of the room, as she slipped off the bathrobe and climbed under the covers.

Katelyn joined in the festivities of the shaman's noon-time celebrations but kept thinking of Anthony. Looking for Gwylin, she wanted to inform her she needed to head back to her campsite and let Anthony know what was transpiring. It seemed everybody but Gwylin was in attendance, and since she and her doppelganger Naldi were the guests of honour at this little soiree, she knew she would be unable to slip away unnoticed.

Taking another sip from the earthen mug as the bitter liquid was proffered, she wondered what it was made from. Pointing at the goblet Katelyn asked Naldi if she knew what it was. Naldi shook her head and smiled but turned to the woman next to her and asked. Turning back to Katelyn, Naldi repeated what she heard: "It is from the flower you call a poppy."

"OK," said Katelyn looking up at the sky, "I don't need visions from Morpheus adding to the already lucid dreamscape I used to call reality." Seeing Gwylin exit the wolfman's hut, she called out to her waving and finally got her to come to the table where she sat.

"Gwylin, I must go and tell Anthony what is happening as he will be worrying about me and I can't relax knowing he is concerned for me."

"Not to worry miss, I sent two boys to bring him here once they find him. There are several others we are also searching for this day who will be tested for suitability to travel into the portal. Tonight is another night of initiation. We have no time to lose now Naldi has returned," said Gwylin, as she looked deeply into her sister's eyes. She looked back to Katelyn and, lifting the cup to her lips, said "Please drink. This will help you stay relaxed for the upcoming journey. At sunset we will be testing your abilities at the portal and at dawn you will step through, if you are worthy and willing."

Katelyn didn't know what to say. Deciding they had been honest and were treating her with respect, although she was still upset at the wolfman for the way he took back the fossil pendant, she thought everything was probably a test, so why fight it. "Thanks", she said, and taking a long drink, drained the contents from the stone cup. Smiling, Gwylin refilled it and said, "Drink slowly this time and after this cup no more." She then filled Naldi's cup from the earthenware pitcher and, after placing it back on the table, walked back to the hut. Before she entered, she turned her head smiling at Katelyn and nodded once.

Katelyn ate a little more of the food they had offered but found the spices nauseating. The gathering was breaking up slowly as many of the folk that weren't laying down in the afternoon sun were stumbling back over the bridge into town. *I need to lie down too,* she thought as she watched the man who owned the bike shop flop onto a comfortable looking patch of grass. *Looks big enough for two* she mused, and decided to join him there.

Anthony rode into town along the main street, turned right onto the short lane beside Davo's shop and entered through the gate into his backyard around lunchtime. He was feeling really good from the bike ride, appreciating the deep connection to nature he felt from the fresh mountain air enlivening his body and mind. He noticed the raft Davo had been repairing earlier was gone. He placed the bike back where he found it and, heading out of town towards camp to see if Katelyn had returned, saw most of the shops were still closed.

Sitting beside his tent were two local boys who sprang to their feet and came running towards him as he approached. They had very serious looks upon their faces and he feared the worst.

"You must come with us," said the taller of the two boys, who Anthony knew to be the ringleader of the little posse he'd seen interacting with the other tourists, "Gwylin has requested that you arrive as soon as possible."

"What's happened, is Katelyn alright? Where is everybody from the town, why are the shops still closed?" he said grabbing the boy by his shoulders.

"Everything is fine sir. Sorry, I did not mean to scare you. Katelyn is okay. My great aunt Naldi has returned," said the boy with a mixture of seriousness and joy twinkling in his eyes. "This is a very special day for us. Great change is coming and Katelyn is a chosen one. This is all I know. Bring some food and warmer clothes. That is all you will need for now."

Anthony continued to look into the boy's eyes to make sure this was a true account, and satisfied with the boy's honesty he moved him aside and continued towards his tent. After selecting a few warmer pieces of clothing and changing his sweaty shirt he told them he would need to go to the storage hut for some food and then they could head to their camp.

"No problem sir, we will come with you," said the shorter of the two boys, smiling broadly, glad to be able to participate and use his English.

"I really would like a shower," said Anthony distractedly, as he changed his running shoes for hiking boots and put on a clean pair of woolen socks.

"No time for a shower sir," said the taller of the two boys, exerting his authority.

"Yes, I know, I was just thinking out loud," replied Anthony, as he thought about what food he could bring. *Why can't they feed me? I'm sure they have food,* he thought, as he decided on what he might want for dinner. He stood, closed the fly on his tent and then reopened it and selected a fresh pair of woolen socks from Katelyn's bag, knowing how much she would appreciate them.

"Let's go," he said, as he walked briskly towards the storage lockers where his supplies were kept.

Gwylin and Bon Chen were talking in an ancient dialect only the chosen were able to understand and since there were no new nag pa in their tribe they were not afraid of being overheard and understood.

Bon Chen's voice sounded deep, like distant thunder, as he expressed his thoughts to Gwylin. "Naldi told me of her journey to Nibiru. She believes the Nephilim are readying themselves for our galactic alignment in six months, and plan to come and visit Earth again. As custodians of the portal we have been preparing for this for hundreds of years and, just as the prophecies are about to come true, our clan is disintegrating. We cannot rely on these pilgrims to fulfill the roles of nag pa just because our kin have left for the cities." Bon Chen was drawing spirals in the dirt at his feet, with the tip of a stick he had pulled from his hut's thatch roof before they squatted down. "They have not been trained properly. My efforts to stimulate their subtle bodies may not be enough." Looking up he saw the same concern in Gwylin's eyes.

"They are all we have," she replied softly, empathizing with Bon Chen's concern but unwilling to lose hope. "If the prophecies are true, then after all the trial and tribulations yet to befall them, they will prevail. We will prevail and the Nephilim will be thwarted in their attempts to subjugate humanity."

Bon Chen looked toward the mountain, "We might need to get the military of all nations involved if we cannot stimulate the portals before alignment occurs. We will soon know if love will truly overcome. Our time is at hand and humanity is still bickering with one another like children squabbling over a favoured toy. I feel there is much change needed in the psyche of humanity and too little time to achieve the levels of consciousness required. Man is a lazy animal. Maybe a threat from the Nephilim will bring us to a better understanding of our place in the Galaxy, or maybe we will be wiped out or replaced like the other hominids of Earth history."

Gwylin was silent while she looked at Katelyn sleeping next to Dochen. She thought of the others she would need to fulfill the prophecy. *They are so young and time is limited.* She looked back to Bon Chen and said, "It might be time for me to enter the portal my friend. It might also be your time."

Bon Chen held her gaze, as a smile started to spread across his face, his *yes* glinting from underneath the muzzle of the wolf head. He burst into uproarious laughter and, after a while, regained his composure. "You know, I believe you are right. It is time we went traveling again. First, we will see what they learn tomorrow."

Angie and Shala had finished their late afternoon lunch and were walking down the front steps of the mess hall when they heard a small woman in a straw hat approaching, pointing her walking stick at them and saying, "Excuse me misses. You need to come with me. As I'm sure you've heard, all visitations to the portal have been suspended until further notice. My clan have some important work to accomplish and you are to be involved." Angie looked at Shala and they both shrugged their shoulders with smiles on their faces. "Destiny," they said in unison, their eyes wide. Turning to face the woman, Shala said:

"Let us return to our tent and exchange some things and prepare. Where will we be sleeping tonight?"

"You will stay with us. There are to be some initial ceremonies and two visits to the portal. You will need warm clothes, a bag of provisions and water. You may be going for a journey tomorrow." She held up her hand, as Angie began to ask her what she was talking about and continued, "I'm sorry, but it will become clearer this evening if you are to be chosen. We are gathering several pilgrims we feel may be up for the task and you will all be tested for suitability. Now go, and then meet me back here as quickly as you can." Gwylin then headed up the stairs and into the mess hall, seeking other potential candidates.

Angie and Shala hurried to their tent, discussing what it all meant, excited to be offered a chance at the portal. "We're extremely fortunate to arrive while there is still a chance to go to the portal. If it's closed to all those who aren't chosen there are going to be some very disappointed people. I hope it doesn't get ugly up there," said Shala, voicing her fears as the magnitude of what was happening became apparent.

"I hear you. I'm hoping all those who arrived with us today are open to the idea they may never get a turn. How are they deciding who is to partake in these ceremonies I wonder?" asked Angie rhetorically, as they arrived at their tent. "How much of a role does synchronicity play in the meaningful unfolding of events like these, or do humans just make the best of whatever situation they can? It feels to me that we really are in the right place at the right time and destiny is at hand. It's very exciting!" exclaimed Angie, and then thought of David talking about synchronicity, *"...since meaning is a complex mental construction, subject to conscious and subconscious influence, not every correlation in the grouping of events by meaning needs to have an explanation in terms of cause and effect. However, the moment and your participation in its unfolding can't be separated and all meaning arises from the connections we make."*

Angie turned to Shala and taking hold of her hands looked into her dark brown eyes and said, "At the end of the day we are here and they are picking us for reasons we can only guess at this stage. Some call it fate, but whatever transpires, soon it will be history and whatever forces are building behind the scenes and whatever reasons we use to justify how it came to be, I get the distinct feeling tomorrow is going to be a big day!"

"I feel the same Angie. I'm so glad you came with me. It's like I'm on a roller-coaster ride and the thrills are getting more intense, but with the excitement comes a fear response that I'm hoping I will continue to stay on top of. Sometimes it feels as though I'm about to get thrown sideways by a force I can't handle. How are you staying so focused Angie?" Shala asked, staring deeply into her green eyes.

Angie again thought of David and repeated what he had told her about synchronicity and Carl Jung's ideas, although it wasn't the whole story. "Jung believed that there are parallels between synchronicity and quantum mechanics. He thought deeply about the idea that life was not a series of random events but rather an expression of a deeper unfolding order. This deeper order meant that a person was both embedded in a framework, was the focus of that framework and that this realization had elements of a spiritual awakening." She looked down the path as two girls came quickly towards them, and waited to see if they were coming to talk to them, but they hurried past, heading on towards their own tent. Continuing, Angie said, "I like to think of it as the dreamer within the dream realizing she is dreaming just in time to save herself from whatever psychological battles she is generating for herself in the sleep state, to test her own mettle."

Angie let go of Shala's hands and finished up by saying, "I think we can talk more about this later and it might be time for me to share some of the deeper experiences that have been happening to me in the last month or so."

Shala kept staring into Angie's eyes and had the sudden realization that Angie was not the girl she thought, seeing for the first time an incredibly powerful woman. "You've been holding out on me babe," she laughed, and lightly punched Angie on the shoulder. "It's fine. I see it now. I've been stuck in my own trip for so long I didn't really notice you changing. I thought it was the flush of love from hooking up with David but this goes way deeper. Anyway you're right. Let's chat after we pack. I'm feeling better just seeing the depth to which you understand the energies affecting us. I will face my fears tonight. Thanks again for being here, you're so awesome," she said, leaping onto Angie with a squeal and giving her a bear hug and finishing by saying, "A faithful heart makes wishes come true."

They packed in silence and walked back to the mess hall where Gwylin was patiently waiting with several other people they recognized from the bus trip. They turned around as the two girls who had passed them earlier, arrived, a mixture of excitement and apprehension in their eyes.

"This is everyone. We must go now," said Gwylin, as she turned and strode away at an alarmingly quick pace for an old woman, in the direction of her home.

Those who hadn't met on the bus ride from Bahraich introduced themselves and they all chatted excitedly about the rendezvous with the portal that was to take place this evening.

Angie looked around and counted three guys including Richard, who still wore the same frown from this morning, along with five girls including herself and Shala. *I wonder how many they are needing? In my dream there were only four girls, two of whom aren't even here. Curious. Maybe they send us through in groups of four?*

They arrived at the shaman's camp as the sun was cresting the top of the mountain on its journey to the underworld, its shadow growing ominously over the assemblage of pilgrims and their new hosts. The wolfman was slinking around and sniffing them in his customary way. Smelling fear in some and acknowledging the potentials. Angie saw the two women from her vision who she thought were sisters, walking towards them with a man she had never seen before.

Shala grabbed Angie by the arm as she too noticed the women approaching, exclaiming through gritted teeth, "Oh my god Angie, that's the woman from my dreams! She's the one, the one who disappears into the mountain."

Gwylin rapped her walking stick on a log and they all turned to face her. "You are to drink a special brew which will help calm your nerves and open you to some of the more subtle energies of the mountain. There will be chanting and dancing after we return from the first period of testing at the portal. It has taken longer than we had hoped to gather you here this evening and we must move quickly…"

"Why the sudden urgency?" asked Pedro. "What has happened? We heard rumours that someone has returned? We need some answers ...please," he added, not wanting to sound too pushy.

Katelyn started to speak and they all turned and faced her as she filled them in on what she had learnt since waking

138

after her nap at lunchtime. "This morning, as my time at the vortex was ending, I saw a face emerging from the kaleidoscope of colours at the entrance to the portal. The face belonged to Naldi," she said, gesturing to Naldi, who stood serenely in the diminishing light of dusk. "Naldi is Gwylin's older sister who entered the portal back in 1961." Murmurs from the others compelled her to raise her hand to silence them and she continued, "She hasn't aged a day, and in her reckoning, was gone about six months. In that time she exited three other portals whose locations I have been unable to ascertain. She brought back a large geode given to her by a tribe who are the guardians of one of the portals. They are possibly Australian from her description, as translated to me. The other two portals she exited were overlooking scenes of wilderness and no-one was there to acknowledge her presence."

"What's a geode?" asked Michaela.

Katelyn answered, "A geode is a crystal encased in rock. You have probably seen them in crystal shops cut open to reveal amethyst and other such minerals inside". Michaela and some of the others nodded their heads. "Anyway, our task if we choose to accept their mission will be to see if we can discover where the other portals are. I have arranged for each group to carry a GPS, although I don't know if the strong energy of the portal will adversely affect the electronics. It was the only way I could think to generate a coordinate." Looking around and seeing no one else had a better suggestion, Katelyn continued. "Legend speaks of eight portals considered to be the vertices of cosmic energies as they generate the planetary grid of Earth. You'll have to bear with me as this is quite esoteric, but once you've experienced the energy of the portal it begins to make more sense."

"This is the planetary merkerba I dreamed of over a month ago," said Shala. "Two interlocking tetrahedrons nested together like two giant pyramids. One standing upright, the other inverted," she described with her hands as she spoke. "Picture a 3D Star of David and you get the idea. Sorry I..."

"No please, if anyone has information, feel free to share. Like I said, this is new to me too. Our friendly wolfman here," she said, gesturing to Bon Chen squatting on his haunches, chewing on a leg of goat left over from lunch, "has his PhD in archaeology from Oxford University and speaks English perfectly." He paid them no attention. "Apparently as we approach the Galactic Alignment of 2012 if these portals aren't open and functioning properly, the Earth will suffer major tectonic displacement resulting in earthquakes, volcanic eruptions and tsunamis on an unprecedented scale. Pretty much all the doomsday scenarios you hear about 2012 would come true if the portals can't handle the harmonics of this galactic alignment. It doesn't bode well on the microcosmic level for humans either. Mental illness will continue to plague humanity as the energies increase. People will need to learn how to move energy through their bodies, if they want to avoid being fried."

"So how do we help energize these portals once we find them?" asked Pedro.

"Good question", replied Katelyn. "Once we have documented their whereabouts, hopefully with the GPS's, large groups of people will then be needed to meditate on the specific geographical regions whilst two individuals, one male and one female, stand in the centre of the portal, connecting with the humans and sending them the necessary vibrational frequencies. Apparently, consciousness is required to travel along electromagnetic wavefronts towards galactic centre. If the black hole at our galactic core doesn't absorb the overtones of sentient beings acting as custodians for the planet, then the planet usually crumbles and turns into a lifeless asteroid field. This is of course the absolute worst case scenario, but according to legend this is what happened to the planet Chiron here in our own solar system eons ago. According to some ,Chiron is the asteroid belt between Mars and Jupiter and mythically is known as the wounded healer".

"It's June twentieth today, and the Solstice is tomorrow, which according to Bon Chen - the wolfman - is a very important precursor to the December Solstice, with only one other maximum power day being the Equinox in September. Six months is all we have to gather all the divergent groups of people who are open to the potential of 2012 and unify them with the single intent of transformation and galactic resonance."

Gwylin interrupted any further questions by saying, "It is time to drink the medicine and make our way to the portal to see who is eligible to go through tomorrow."

David and Angie had spent their final night together discussing some of the broader ideas of consciousness transformation and the harmonics of the 'hologram of hyperspace' as David liked to refer to reality.

They were sitting on the bed, feeding each other pieces of lightly seared tuna and sipping warm saki. "When I felt myself as the fractal edge of universal mind, I could see myself as though I was part of a living Mandelbrot set. You're familiar with that particular fractal?" Angie nodded her head. "So as you know, you can zoom into any part of the image and keep going deeper and deeper and deeper and eventually you find yourself zooming into what looks like the same place you started. We know of this as self-similarity. Now, what is so beautiful about the Mandelbrot fractal to me is how humanoid the initial figure appears. I mean it takes a little imagination but not much, to picture yourself as the Buddha-beetle-thing, right?" he finished, laughing at himself as he tried to describe it.

"Yes, I know exactly what you're describing, but how does the fractal image fit in with the idea of a hologram and how does it all tie back to hyperspace?" replied Angie, as they ate more pieces of the succulent tuna.

"It's hard to picture without looking at the images on a computer screen or the formulas if you're a mathematician, but using an analogy from Eastern Mysticism, think of Aum, the primordial sound. What they are identifying, in their prescientific way, is that the universe is made of vibration. We discussed holograms a few weeks back and you understand they are generated by two sources of coherent light creating an interference pattern; the same way two stones thrown into a pond create two separate sets of ripples. When those two sets of ripples intersect, they generate a new formation of waves, which is the amalgamation of the original two. We have the idea of the Mother and Father principal or Yin and Yang or positive and negative. The mother and father come together and their union creates the child. It is the product of the union of the two polar opposites we are interested in.

We don't know how the universe came into being but what exists right here right now can be experienced using the technology of the human body and consciousness. We can know what it is to be the universe because we are the product of the mother and father principle in action. We are a microcosm of the universe. We are the universal child. Like Joseph Campbell used to say, "We are the hero with a thousand faces." If we can understand the myths and legends, we can experience what it all points to."

The sat in silence for a while, looking into each others eyes and watching each other's faces morph through a myriad of archetypal images. "The difficult part is picturing what is sustaining the hologram we call reality. One needs to imagine they are a hologram. We are essentially empty space and what we call matter is the interference pattern of the archetype. I think that's the best place to start mathematical relationships of ideas. There's no point pretending there are two huge lasers somewhere out in space, but working with Jung's idea of archetypes adds that level of understanding. Archetypes are supposed to have been present in folklore and literature for thousands of years. The origins of the archetypal hypothesis date back as far as Plato and his ideas of pure mental forms, which are like imprints in the mind. They are collective in the sense that they embody the fundamental characteristics of an idea rather than its specific peculiarities. Putting all this together is about opening up to the grander levels of what it means to be one with Creation. This is where an understanding of how fractals are generated through simple algorithms, and how holograms are created through the simple process of interference, is really just the beginning in helping people access new levels for communing with reality." David stopped talking and took another sip of saki.

"I really think it's the pictures that activate me the most. I also watched the video you mentioned, zooming in on the Mandelbrot fractal, and feel I have a greater understanding of what you are describing. Starting at the outer level and imagining the black-beetle-Buddha-thing as the Milky Way

Galaxy and then zooming in until you come to our solar system, then keep going until you reach planet Earth, then zoom in further until you find us sitting in a building on the edge of the planet and then fly in further still to our cells and then on into our molecules and then down to atoms. It helped me to get a good grasp of what you are describing when visualizing these levels of scale and then overlaying it with my understanding of our place in the bigger picture. it sems to be all about boundaries or surface and our definitions of these edges." Angie paused for a moment to collect her thoughts. "How do you share the experience of chakras opening and consciousness flowing through your meridians, with people who have never known such a thing?" she concluded, as she picked up a piece of pickled ginger and placed it on her tongue.

"I wish you weren't leaving tomorrow Angie. I love these conversations and it's wonderful having someone to bounce my ideas off. This is exactly the part of the puzzle I'm not sure how to place. I am a scientist. I can show my theories and use math and data to add weight to my case but opening someone to the idea that they have chakras, and how it is in their best interest to work on opening them is very difficult. Even with pictures, kundalini, prana and an understanding of ourselves as beings of pure energy, can be difficult to relate to.

I mention the topology of hyperspace in my book and describe how waves heterodyne; small waves riding on larger waves and those waves riding and harmonizing with even larger waves. If people could truly grasp all the wavelengths of the electromagnetic spectrum and how they resonate, then maybe that would be another way to help them move from their localized idea of being into a greater appreciation for the scale at which waves of energy are nesting, in order to sustain us and everything around us in this moment.

I mean it's bizarre. We are ripples in the fabric of space. Space that we now measure to be about thirteen billion light years old; space that is 97% empty. What we call matter, created by exploding stars, coalesced with mathematical precision into waves sustaining the form we can look at in a mirror. Maybe this saki is going to my head and I'm not making much sense, but it's all so clear to me. No matter how I think of it, it's hard for me to look at creation any other way." David stopped talking, closed his eyes and took a few deep breaths.

More composed, he continued, "When I look at a mountain range I see the mathematics of the fractal algorithm that generates it. When I look at a tree or a pinecone or a pineapple or a flower, I see the mathematics of the algorithm that generates it. It kind of reminds me how in the movie The Matrix, Neo sees the binary data cascading in front of his eyes. I see the waves and how they heterodyne. I see the harmonics and the fine structure interplay of light and sound required to keep those wavefronts from collapsing through disharmony."

David opened his eyes and looked at the last few pieces of seared tuna and, cocking his head and raising an eyebrow, silently asked Angie if she was going to partake. She shook her head no, in response. David then speared a healthy looking piece with one chopstick and brought it to his mouth like an ancient Greek senator about to eat a bunch of grapes, and took a bite of the succulent flesh. Closing his eyes again, he savoured the taste before continuing. "Sacred geometry from older civilizations was an attempt at describing their understanding of the nature and role of scale and self-similarity and its harmonic relational parameters. I like the metaphors of fractals and holograms for our time as well."

He took another bite of tuna. "The importance of understanding the models we have, whether they be new or old, has a profound effect on whether we will be able to ride these subtler vibrations into an experience of hyperspace. This is a change in consciousness. A change in how we perceive and experience reality. Like Einstein said, 'You cannot solve a problem from the same consciousness that created it'. If our experience of life is limited, then we need to open to a grander vision of ourselves."

Angie knew exactly what David was saying. *I too see the fabric of reality shimmering before my eyes. I know my body is a vibrating field of energy.* "You mentioned the solstice at the end of this year as a transformational opportunity. What is the science behind the rhetoric?" she asked before taking another small sip of saki.

With his eyes still closed, David said, "To put it simply, matter exists where the nodes of interference are. We call them standing waves. The Sun exists where there is a massive harmonic node within the galactic field; a dwell point for gravity. The planets are massive harmonic nodal points also. Our bodies are microcosmic nodal points. The centre of the Milky Way Galaxy is a super massive nodal point. When these nodes are phase locked by their harmonic alignment in December, our consciousness will be able to travel along the larger waves connecting all the harmonics of our galaxy. The subtle waveform of consciousness will resonate with all the wavefronts that comprise the hologram we call reality and, using our body as the instrument to experience totality, we will perceive the world anew.

Connection with Universal Mind - the macrocosm - is achieved through harmonizing your body - the microcosm - with the whole system. The science of this nesting, is the language of light. Quantum electro-dynamics is as close as Western science can get to understanding this field of connectedness, from the very small to the very large. Cybernetics is the study of the system of this feedback mechanism." David opened his eyes and Angie saw galaxies whirling like snowflakes in a snowstorm in the blackness of his irises.

David reached into his trouser pocket and pulled out his black notebook. "I wrote a short story about you. I call it a nano-story it's so short. I would like to share it. I have been thinking about the changes that await our species as the eschatological event horizon of this upcoming Solstice approaches. You are the character Yinn and the story is called My Shining Star.

Yinn rippled silently; shimmered if you had the ability to perceive. A download. Yinn had that all too familiar feeling, like goose bumps in the old world, hairs raised in expectation. The tingling always felt good, no matter what the trigger. Virus scan, cool no contagions. Mnemonics was a risky business and always had been. Never spare the messenger. Encryption was vastly improved these days but still, when you carry the sort of information that pays well, you expect trouble.

At twenty-seven Yinn was an old hand. She'd been in the game since she was seventeen. Straight off she was a natural. She had a purity for information storage that was rare; she felt it and knew to charge accordingly. She had never been out of work and was usually carrying three or more R.O.T.E.s at any one time. Receipt of Total Experience

(R.O.T.E.), the complete data exchange mechanism; no compression.

Yinn was a special breed; the first batch after Hyper-fuse. All the old systems crashed; imploded. No good to be so self-referential that you become your own Singularity. No one predicted antigravity anomalies on the micro-scale of individuals but we should have seen it coming. The math had been there for ages. At least it wasn't an anticlimax like the millennium-bug!

The new breed; self-aware occupiers of hyperspace, navigators riding toroids of the Nth dimension, and we used to think a couple of G's was hard-core. Intent. That's all it was. Focused will. But how do you achieve escape velocity as mind only? Well, that is the trick. Some people, kids like Yinn mostly, don't even think twice about it. Poor old adults with all their knowledge, never prepared them for anything like this. The New Age Movement was the worst affected. They didn't realize the truth of their-own rhetoric; fried by the feedback-loop of anticipation. Which instant is it exactly, when you realize you're IT; the End, the Beginning and everything in between? It's got to hurt, frying yourself because as a simple reflex-capacitor you forgot to discharge.

Yinn decoded rendezvous coordinates for the next download and dissolved. That was everybody's favourite - translocation - easy when you know how. Just don't resist occupying space elsewhere; travel without movement. Funny how science never quite got it together either. Teleportation, their holy grail. Big joke, them thinking they discovered the Unified Field Theory, only to realize after all those catastrophic experiments that the numeral zero really was an anomaly in recursive systems. The irony. I love it. When nothing matters. It was so Zen they couldn't fathom it. The hyper-spatial haiku: How many theoretical physicists does it take to count...? ZERO!

Yinn picked up her new job and did some banking. Only a few more mega-credits and she was retiring. No more messenger girl. No more humping other peoples' shit around. To be clean... to be free. To be the multifaceted jewel of human expression without the greasy layers of corporate espionage. To be pure primal-tone-Yinn. Holofracticly self-perpetuating to infinity; one with the Universal matrix. No boundaries!

Her contract was nearly over. The hyperbole of her own future made her dizzy; so much velocity to an expansion of this magnitude. Very few humans had gone supernova and no one had the capacity to run their R.O.T.E.s anyway. Hyper-hyperbole, that's how Yinn contained the focus. Then, in a flash she was gone. Mega-credit limit reached. Final job uploaded.

I cried for days. I was so happy. See you Yinn. I love you!'"

David looked up from his notebook and into Angie's eyes as he finished and could see the glistening of tears forming.

"That was beautiful," she said, as she leant forward and kissed him on the lips. "I love you too," she whispered, their noses and foreheads touching. "I want to shine with you in hyperspace".

David received an early morning phone call from a research assistant, two days after Angie had left for India, inviting him to Chichen Itza, the Mayan step pyramid in the jungles of Mexico. His associate had measured an energy anomaly within what was previously believed to be a solid structure.

"What's the story, Hans?" David asked, still coming to wakefulness, having been roused from a deep sleep. He rolled over and, turning on the bedside lamp, looked at the time on his Rolex. His friend Hans, who had been following leads David had generated in his theories on Earth's harmonic network, had been to most of the ancient Mayan ruins around the Yucatan Peninsula. Using all types of different electronic devices for measuring energy disturbances, he had found small fluctuations at several of the old sites, but nothing like this one. David got out of bed and headed for the kitchenette.

"I have spent the last three days walking around the step pyramid on each one of its levels measuring some very high readings with the sonograph. The frequencies are between 22khz and 23khz, which is an extremely small spread. I think they built this pyramid directly around a very high frequency vortex. When I reached the top, the energy had lessened considerably, but there is a noticeable spike at the GM ratio. Also there is a steel plate over an opening on the northern side. The plate has been welded into place and apparently there is a narrow set of stairs that lead to a chamber inside. I am having a couple of the elders who informed me of this, petition the National Institute of Anthropology and History, the current caretakers of the site, to let us do some research. When can you get here?" Hans finished asking, as David poured some orange juice into a glass.

David put the juice container back in the fridge, took a small sip and said, "Book me a flight and email me the itinerary. I'll be there as soon as you can get me there."

Hans Zimmerman was wearing his khaki fatigues, looking like a German version of the Crocodile Hunter, when David met him at Cancun airport the following afternoon. Tall and lean with a swatch of close-cropped blonde hair and piercing blue eyes, Hans was the picture of Hitler's skewed vision of the perfect human; an *ubermensch*.

They drove out to Chichen Itza in Hans' rented midnight blue Acura RDX. "We were able to secure a one week access permit to the site. They've cordoned off the pyramid to tourists, claiming maintenance and safety reasons. We had to pay for their loss in revenue but I think this could be one of the major vortices your theory predicted." Hans kept looking over at David to see his reaction. "You don't seem as excited as I thought you would be David," he concluded, his own energy deflating somewhat.

"Sorry Hans. I am very excited. I just want to experience it for myself, before I start jumping to conclusions or saying that it vindicates my theories. I certainly appreciate your level of enthusiasm. My concern is that we are able to keep this a secret until we can verify what we are dealing with. Before I flew down I did more research into the energy anomaly in Nepal where my friends are headed, the one that hit the popular press recently and is being called the Portal of Creation." Hans nodded his head. "I just want to make sure we know what we're dealing with here."

Hans had to slow the car, as two cows wandered across the road up ahead. "I also did some more research on the pyramid itself. In the 1930s, the Mexican government sponsored an excavation and discovered a staircase under the north side of the pyramid. Digging down, they found another temple buried below the current one and inside the temple chamber was a jade throne in the shape of a Jaguar, inlaid with gold. The room had been open to the public for nearly fifty years after that, but in the early part of 2003 tourists started getting ill from effects while standing in the chamber." Hans brought the car to a stop and sounded the horn as the two cows stood staring at them for several minutes before deciding to continue on their way. "Many of the tourists reported visions of sacrifices and mentioned experiencing synaesthetic effects of hearing colours and seeing sounds, from sources which could not be identified. In 2006 the National Institute of Anthropology and History closed the throne room and it hasn't been opened since."

They drove in silence for several miles. "Based on the modeling I have done, the vortexes of energy are cyclic phenomena moving with the precession of the equinoxes. They seem to wax and wane every two thousand years or so, with smaller epicycles in between. We of course are heading to a galactic alignment in six months, during the summer solstice in this part of the world, and as you know, this particular pyramid is designed to capture the solstice sunrise and show the return of the fabled Plumed Serpent on that day. The fact that their calendar also moves onto the next Baktun is more than a coincidence."

David was silent for the rest of the drive, the importance of a portal at this particular geographical location playing out scenarios in his mind. *This alignment hasn't occurred for almost 26,000 years.* He thought of the myths of Genesis and the anthropological data verifying humanity's creation at the hands of the gods, *but who were they exactly, how did they get here and where did they go? Who or what is*

Quezacotl, the deity who is prophesied to return? He pondered his theory that wormholes and space-travel were tied to these vortexes of energy and decided he should contact Eamon, his friend in Egypt and have him go back into the chambers of Cheops.

The group of potentials, hand picked by Gwylin, stood in a line outside the entry to the portal as the sun, a blazing fire-orange orb, was setting over the snow capped mountains to the West. They had been instructed to move towards the railing in front of the vortex of colours, one at a time. They were to approach the railing slowly and remain there for a few minutes, opening themselves to whatever emotions, thoughts and sensations they could experience. If at anytime they felt nauseated, they were to come back to the entrance and the next person would enter, giving the aspirant time to adjust to the powerful energy of the vortex.

There were nine foreigners in total. The five that Anthony had taken to Davo's this morning - Holly, Pedro, Enrique, Michaela and Mary – as well as Shala, Angie, Katelyn, and Richard. Gwylin had considered Anthony as an option but there seemed too much psychic confusion for him to handle. *He certainly is sensitive enough but his saviour Jesus seems too distracting for him currently.* Anthony had gone back to his camp to pray for their safety and said he would return before Katelyn was to step through in the morning.

Each of the chosen had their time near the portal without incident. Katelyn experienced the same heightened body sensations as she had this morning, but noticed thoughts of apprehension in her willingness to step through tomorrow. *I can't be gone for fifty years. I need complete certainty we can return within the month.*

Angie and Shala had been discussing the same prospect as they had hiked to the portal earlier in the evening. Angie spoke to Shala over her shoulder as they made their way with the others across the small wooden bridge. "If Naldi was gone fifty years on this side of the portal but only half a year on the other side, I calculated that every day we spend in there, if we decide to step through, is comparable to three months on this side. Therefore we have less than two days on the other side before the solstice and galactic alignment in December, six months from now, is over and our mission redundant."

Shala thought about the implications of this as she also focused on keeping her balance crossing the rickety little wooden bridge, whilst watching the waters churning beneath her feet. Reaching the other bank Shala let out a deep sigh and said, "We need to know more about the implications of time distortion from the perspective of the other side. It's a shame Naldi can't speak better English. Actually, why doesn't the wolfman explain to us more of what's going on? I think we need to ask some serious questions when we return this evening. I'm with you. If we step through..."

Gwylin had been listening to their concerns and felt the others also beginning to harbour doubts. Cutting off Shala by raising her voice, she said, "Your job is to find and energize the other portals and hopefully make contact with the custodians of these portals, if any of them are left. Naldi took so long on the other side because she could not find her way back to this portal. We needed a specific frequency carrier and no one in our tribe matched. Katelyn proved to be the one we had been waiting for." She called out to the others to stop walking and

154

gathered them together in the field of yellow and purple flowers. "Please sit down for a few moments and I will explain quickly a few more details. You cannot carry so much confusion with you into the field of the vortex."

Leaning on her walking stick, Gwylin looked at each one of them in turn. "I have selected you from many potentials who come here. You are all very clear beings. Your intentions are noble and singular. You have open hearts and seek truth above all else. I can see your chakras and know you will be able to harmonize with the energies of the portal. The task we ask of you has been something all of you have been preparing yourselves for over many months. You are drawn to do this, as you know deep down it is your destiny. We haven't much time, as the energy will peak tomorrow and will then start to wane and not peak again until the Equinox. Time is relative inside the energy of the portal. When the portal is at maximum energy, time on both sides is equal, but as it wanes there is an accelerating dilation of time between the two realms. Naldi was never told of this, as it only complicates the psyche of the nag pa." Gwylin glanced up at the sunshine glistening on the very tips of the snowy peaks to the East. "Please, you will enter in the morning and return within the day if all goes according to plan." With this said, she whacked Pedro on his thigh with her walking stick and with a friendly chuckle urged them on.

Katelyn, stood at the portal recalling the words Gwylin had said to encourage them, "…if all goes according to plan." *Not very reassuring,* she mused as she turned and walked back out of the cave. It was getting dark outside and the light from the bank of LED's cast a ghostly glow upon their faces, as they stood on the ledge around the entrance. Combined with the drop in temperature, lack of food and the somnambulistic after effects of the poppy tea, the chosen were all feeling less than euphoric as they waited silently ruminating their private thoughts and reading uncertainty in their fellow nag pa.

Shala and Angie had been staring into each other's eyes trying to fathom the other's emotions. Angie felt peaceful and Shala was glad to be able to feel her friend's peace, amongst the fleeting thoughts of uncertainty that flittered like moths inside her own mind.

Angie had learned to contain, modulate and direct the energies flowing within her body over the past month, keeping the flow of her consciousness calm and positive. Her experience at the portal was one of deep insight into the potential unfolding for humanity; the energies of Earth's alignment with the galactic core entailed great change. She did not have visions of cataclysm and catastrophe but on the contrary, had a vision of forgiveness sweeping the world like a Mexican Wave at the World Cup. People throwing their arms into the air rejoicing, then embracing one another with love and compassion.

They headed back to camp for more initiations before tomorrow's ultimate decision. To step through or not step through? - that was the question.

Chapter Seven - Soul Mining

Wollumbin is the lava core of an extinct volcano, which erupted many millions of years ago. The mountain remains a place of cultural significance to the Bunjalung people and is the site of particular ceremonies and initiation rites. The local tribe still observes traditional restrictions prohibiting the uninitiated from climbing the mountain. Located not far inland from the popular tourist destination of Byron Bay, Wollumbin's secret has been difficult to maintain. Several aboriginal men of the Bunjalung tribe are always present but never seen by tourists, who come from all over the world to climb her forested slopes and revel in the majestic view from her summit.

An opening on the western slope not far below the summit leads back into a central lava tube and down to the object of the tribe's continued need for secrecy; a portal. When Naldi exited this portal she was met by the local gatekeepers and given the geode to aid her journey home. She had stayed with them for several weeks while they initiated her into their tribe as one who was foretold, with dancing, singing and feasting. The songs spoke of travelers exiting the mountian from distant lands when the tribes of the world were to unite in the dawning of a New Age. They also spoke of the possible return of the wrathful creator gods.

It was into the bright orange glare of the setting sun on a brisk evening of Australia's winter solstice that Angie, Shala, Katelyn and Naldi emerged on the western side of Wollumbin. They could hear drumming coming from the summit as they stood looking out onto the massive caldera surrounding them, breathing unfamiliar smells, hearing unseen animals scurrying and a symphony of raucous bird song.

"I'm glad the sun is still shining," said Shala, eyes wide and arms raised, breathing in an appreciation of the beauty of the moment. "Where are we?"

Katelyn turned on the GPS to see if it still worked. "Cool. Location logged. Sorry but we can't delay, we need to head to the next portal. GPS says *Mt. Warning* and in brackets *Wollumbin, Northern NSW, Australia,*" she concluded, placing the GPS back in her pack and then bringing out her canteen and taking a small sip of glacier water.

"Crazy. My watch says it has taken less than ten minutes since we entered the other portal half a world away. This is definitely the way to travel!" exclaimed Shala, turning on her headlamp as they turned and headed back into the mountainside. There were ochre drawings on the walls of the cave which they had not noticed on their way out.

"I've read about these figures," said Shala, as she stopped momentarily and traced her left hand over one of the bulbous heads. "They're called *Wandjina* and are creator spirits, I believe. Look, here is the Rainbow Serpent, the Australian aborigine's major creator deity. I would love to hear some stories from the local tribe," she said this as she walked, outlining the long snake as it undulated on the cave's wall, heading back towards the portal.

Within moments of entering the portal in the belly of Wollumbin, they exited into another sunset and took a reading on the GPS. From the description next to the coordinates, Katelyn read, "The Bandiagara Escarpment. Home of the Dogon who live in a series of natural tunnels weaving through the escarpment." They all looked at each other with expressions of interest and acknowledgement. Turning to Naldi, Katelyn confirmed with a nod and raised eyebrows, gesturing towards the expanse of jungle below them that this was one of the areas she had visited previously. Naldi smiled and nodded in acquiescence.

"Back into the vortex and let's see if we can find the final portal for this journey," said Angie, as they reentered the tunnel through a narrow opening. After each had stepped through the meniscus of colours, they assembled in an area no larger than an elevator with the energies of the portal swirling all around them. Although the energy was intense from the outside, once inside the portal there was an eerie calm and absolutely no sound. It was difficult to talk, as words had little medium to support their existence. Intuition proved a better tool and their subtle body-language spoke volumes in the state of heightened awareness they were all experiencing.

To walk into the centre of the vortex took several disorienting steps, like swimming in a rainbow whirlpool but the portal in the middle was an area beyond normal space and time. They were able to exit in a new direction, as Naldi had drawn Sanskrit text in the dirt around the perimeter of the floor during her previous excursions. Although the four directions marked the four portals she had been through, including the one in the mountain towering over her village, Naldi could not be certain their egress would coincide with an earthly destination. She had spoken at length with Bon Chen earlier that day about the other planet she had visited.

Like the points on a compass, between the cardinal directions of North, South, East and West, there are four more directions, coinciding with North-East, South-East, North-West and South-West. It is one of these points which had taken Naldi beyond our solar system.

Nearing the moment of Solstice, whereby the Sun hangs in the sky at its furthest latitude north of the equator, the portal energies increased in intensity to such a degree, that when Shala looked at her companions, she saw luminous beings of light made of fine plasma filaments like gossamer threads of static electricity. "You guys look like an Alex Grey painting!" she shouted across the vacuum-like space of their enclave.

No one heard a sound as Naldi disappeared once more heading out of the void.

Naldi emerged into a room lit by a neon strip-light attached to a car battery, sitting on what looked to be a hand carved jade throne and knew she had not been here before. As the others arrived behind her she heard the rumble of approaching voices echoing down a passageway and gestured for them to hide behind the throne. Crouching behind Katelyn, Angie watched in disbelief as David entered the room, calling out measurements on a small electronic device he held in his right hand. Angie leapt to her feet, and stepped out from behind the ancient seat of power.

David could not believe his eyes. "What in the world? You've come through from Nepal?" Angie's smile spread ear to ear. She turned and introduced Katelyn and Naldi to David and he said hello to Shala who he'd met before.

Turning to Hans, who was standing behind him, with a look of shock and awe on his face at what he was hearing, David introduced the girls and said, "Well that answers one question." Looking down at his sonograph he continued, "The frequency spread is wider and the signal is at its strongest, since we have been measuring it these last two days." David read out some numbers which Hans copied into a notebook, and then switched off the device. "Let's all head outside, the morning is beautiful."

Katelyn had turned on the GPS and was saving the coordinates. Shala turned to her and quietly asked where they were.

"It says we're in Mexico, at Chitchen Itza, to be precise," Katelyn replied.

"When did you come to Mexico?" Angie asked David, as the six of them stood there coming to grips with the coincidental magnitude of bumping into each other.

Katelyn interrupted David before he started to respond and voiced her concerns about time dilation. "We don't want to spend too long here, until we know for sure the differences in time between each transition."

Angie turned back to Daivd, and asked "What is the date and time?" He looked at his watch and said, "Local time is ten minutes past seven in the morning on June 21, 2012. When did you guys enter the portal in Nepal?"

"We entered about fourty-five minutes ago. Late evening of June 21. We were going to leave early in the morning, but several of the other travelers who were to assist us freaked out as we were about to step through. In the end the four of us have gone to each portal, although…" Turning to Naldi and Katelyn, Angie asked Naldi about this portal. "You haven't been here before, have you?"

"No," Naldi replied, a look of veiled fear shining from her dark brown eyes.

"What is it Naldi?" Angie asked, sensing something was wrong.

"I cannot say. So sorry. We should go. No time to lose."

Angie looked back to David, the pain evident to the others that separating was not what either intended. "I will leave my canteen bottle at the exit point that marks the portal into Nepal. If you wish to come through and take some readings," she said with a smile, breaking the emotional tension of the moment.

"Yes, that sounds like a good idea." He gave her a quick kiss and they all said their goodbyes and walked back through the shimmering rainbow of colours into the portal beyond. David turned to Hans and said, "Let's go back outside. I need to think about what to do next."

Standing at the top of the massive step pyramid of Chitchen Itza, David looked beyond the ruins spread below them barely visible in the early morning light, and to the forest beyond. Thoughts were fighting for privileges in his mind; a rumble in the jungle and he was unsure as to who would win. He was thinking of the other portals and knew the only way forward was to enter and learn from experience what to do next. His theories opened possibilities he was unwilling to acknowledge at this point. It was one thing extrapolating on ideas with no evidence to support the conclusions you could draw, but another thing entirely when your theories suddenly became real.

David turned to Hans. "I need to step through and follow Angie to learn more of what is going on. That woman dressed in the Nepalese clothes knows things we need to understand. Hans are you interested in coming with me or..."

"This is most exciting David, I will be glad to come through at least for one day. I don't feel this to be a problem. We just need to explain to the directors at..."

"Sorry but there is no time. I am going through now. We can leave a note explaining the situation. I don't want to get into a debate with NIAH. I would rather apologize upon my return than be denied permission and have to go against their will." David looked at Hans unequivocally.

"Time to depart?" Hans asked as he patted David on the shoulder.

They entered the pyramid and walked back down the narrow passageway into the chamber, collected the sonograph, their headlamps, and a blanket, which David stuffed into his backpack. He then scanned the small room one more time, picked up a piece of rope, handed one end to Hans and after tying the other end around his waist, moved towards the vortex.

They arrived in the silence of the centre of the portal, both of them feeling highly nauseated. David quickly scanned the perimeter with his headlamp and found Angie's plastic water bottle standing on the dirt floor beside some Sanskrit symbols he could not decipher. Turning back to Hans who was looking very pale, David indicated he was going to step through. Hans took a deep breath and followed as the rope pulled tight.

David burst through into the cave illumined by LED's and crashed straight into the metal safety barrier. Hans dodged around David, jumped the fence, undid the rope from around his waist, ran outside and vomited down the side of the mountain. David joined Hans out on the ledge in the cool night air, taking several deep breaths to ease the giddiness he was feeling. Stars were shining wanly above them and they could see the light of the moon glowing like a halo over the mountain to the East.

"We definitely need some preparation before we do that again," said Hans, as he stood up and wiped his chin. "I bet I'm the first person to vomit genuine Mexican food in Nepal." David looked at him and they both smiled.

"A little travel sickness never hurt anyone." Looking down at the dark swath of the river as it snaked its way along the valley floor, surrounded by groups of campfire light, David said, "Lets head down to the village, see if we can find the girls and get some water. I'm really thirsty. How are you feeling now?"

"I'm feeling better," said Hans before clearing his throat and then spitting. "My head is throbbing, and I have a disgusting taste in my mouth, but I'm fine."

After making their way down the side of the mountain as the twilight faded, they followed the well-trodden path towards the lights of town. Arriving at the mess hall and finding no one outside, they climbed the stairs and pushed open the wooden door into a room full of people talking in many different languages. Between David and Hans they could speak seven languages fluently and heard snippets of conversations about the portal. Many of them were complaining about not being able to go up to visit the portal and lamenting their decisions to come all the way here and then to be denied. Some were discussing different aspects of gossip that had started to develop surrounding the significance of what was unfolding. *You haven't seen anything yet my friends,* thought David, as he made his way amongst them.

The two of them walked around the hall looking for Angie and her fellow travelers but didn't find them. "They don't seem to be here," said David, as they arrived back at the front door. "I don't think it would be wise to mention their names in this crowd tonight. I heard two men speaking Portuguese, berating themselves over their cowardice. These are not happy campers."

Hans agreed and suggested they head further down river towards the lights of town. "I wonder what the time is here. Sometime after dinner by the looks of it," he concluded, noting the smell of food that had been recently cooked and consumed, but seeing no evidence of unwashed bowls on any of the tables.

"At a guess I would say around 6pm due to the fact that Nepal is about eleven hours ahead of Mexico" said David, descending the stairs outside, as two girls walked towards them. "Hello. Can either of you tell me about the women who went into the portal today. Do you know where they might be?"

"There are rumours they went into the portal but I'm not sure I believe it. They're at the shaman's camp I imagine. They've been there since after lunch yesterday as far as we know. It's all very hush hush around here. There are some guys and girls who were at the shaman's camp earlier but they're not talking much either. If you want to know more I suggest going to their camp and asking them."

"Where is their camp?" asked David.

"Sorry, we just arrived," finished Hans, by way of apology. The girls looked at one another, raising their eyebrows. He noticed his comment didn't help matters.

With a look of suspicion in their eyes, the girls looked them up and down, and, noticing they were in shorts and shirts, the girl who hadn't yet spoken asked, "How is it you've just arrived?"

David contemplated lying but couldn't really think of a credible story, so decided the truth might be the best option. "We came through the portal. There are several dotted around the planet and you will be hearing more about them in the coming months, no doubt. I am sorry, but we are in a great hurry, so if you could please explain how to get to the shaman's camp that would be most helpful," he stated efficiently, layering in as much charm and goodwill as possible.

"Sorry, I did not mean to pry, it is none of my business, but that is exciting news." The girl then explained which path to take, said goodbye and watched them leave, before running up the stairs into the mess hall and shouting to everyone inside that two men had come through from another portal. The mood inside the mess hall changed in an instant, and the girls found themselves the centre of attention and the focus of many questions, few of which they could answer.

Hans and David used their headlamps and following the simple directions, crossed the river and made their way into the shaman's camp. As they entered the clearing they noticed a fire with human silhouettes crouched around it, and approaching them, David called out, "Hello!" Several of the figures came to their feet, one ran off to their left, disappearing into a hut while two others came to them.

"Who are you?" asked one of the men.

"We are here to talk to the women who entered the portal today. We have some important information for them," said David, before his attention was diverted by Angie calling out to him from beside the hut.

David and Hans had been invited into Bon Chen's hut after Angie had introduced them to Gwylin and explained as best she could where they had come from.

"Why haven't any Mayans come with you?" asked Gwylin, as they all sat in silence around Bon Chen's small fire.

However it was Katelyn who answered. "As I mentioned earlier it seems many of the other custodians have been unable to maintain their connection with the portals." She turned to David and said, "I believe our next aim should be to connect with these tribes who have been the keepers of the other portals. Of the two other portals we exited, one was in Australia and the other in Africa. We heard drumming coming from the mountaintop in Australia but I think it was tourists, not tribe members. The portal in Africa should be presided over by the Dogon tribe according to the GPS."

David's eyes lit up with this revelation. "I know nothing of the Australian connection, but the Dogon are a very interesting tribe with some curious rituals, which I will not go into here. Suffice it to say, amongst certain anthropologists, they are known for their connection with the binary star system of Sirius and many of their rituals tell stories of the gods who came from that solar system at the dawning of humankind."

Bon Chen translated for Naldi as he knew she could not follow all that had been said. Gwylin, Bon Chen and Naldi looked at one another for several minutes contemplating if they should share with the others more of what Naldi had experienced. Finally, with the slightest of nods of acknowledgement from Gwylin, Bon Chen preceded to tell the story of Naldi's journey to the planet with two suns.

They all listened in astonishment as Bon Chen recounted the history of the inhabitants who had come from the far off planet circling the twin suns of Sirius, their arrival in Egypt, Africa, the Americas and Australia. He told them, how, through their advanced understanding of genetics, they had created the human race from interbreeding existent hominids they found on the various continents. They also created hybrid beings, using their own genetics, who were then left behind to rule over humanity.

He spoke of many of the popular myths, including the Great Flood and the fall of ancient civilizations, as the demigods battled amongst themselves through the vast epochs of time. He spoke of the archaeological artifacts of Sumeria; thousands and thousands of clay tablets, only a fraction of which had been studied and deciphered, detailing stories predating those in the book of Genesis.

After Bon Chen had finished David quietly quoted the bible verse from Genesis 6:4: "The Nephilim were on the Earth in those days, and also afterward, when the sons of God came into the daughters of men, and they bore children to them. These were the mighty men of old, the men of renown."

Epilogue - Return of the Gods

Enki stood facing his half-brother Enlil in the throne room of their father's pyramid. His father Anu - Supreme Lord of the Sky - sat lazily upon his throne, sipped occasionally from a stone mug of sweet mead, cupped by the fingers of his right hand. His left had twirled the hilt of his jewel encrusted gold ceremonial sword, its tip pirouetting silently on the marble floor while he ruminated on the strategies and attitudes his two sons presented - Enki full of compassion, Enlil full of loathing. Anu had little love for the human creatures of Earth and had manipulated most of the animosity between his sons for his own agendas, but the long passage of time had lessened his resolve to continue his galactic ambitions.

He took a large gulp of the mead and licked his lips after swallowing the overly sweet beverage. *Maybe it is time I let go of this ancient plot,* he considered as he placed the now empty goblet on the carved arm of his jade throne and brushed a recalcitrant grey curl from his view. *Enlil has served me well in our other dominions,* he thought as he studied the younger of his heirs.

I could grant Enki his wish. I do not understand his love for those insipid beings. They are so weak minded. I would almost rather see them exterminated. However, their vulnerability is somewhat endearing. I grow soft in my old age.

Standing to Anu's left, Enki, unperturbed by the nefarious plots of his younger brother, was wading in the depths of his own thoughts. *I will have my time on Earth before his legion is loosed. If only father could support me in my final mission before their Galactic Alignment. If I cannot help the chosen in achieving their harmonic resonance, all my efforts for my human children will have been for nought. I so dearly wish to see my Earthly kin gain their immortal independence and enter the galactic body. They are so close. Six moons and their alignment could free them. If Enlil gets his way, his legion of soldiers will destroy any chance they have of accessing the source and key to their own nobility.*

Enlil glared at his brother, his right hand gripping tightly the hilt of his short sword. Always dressed in his battle fatigues, his agenda of retribution on the humans was for him already a forgone conclusion. *Whatever my father decides I will take my men to Earth in those final moments. Armageddon will be my legacy!*

End of Book One.